N

Ass

Journey to Freedom

Art Lester

ISBN: 978-1-326-44204-0

PublishNation, London
www.publishnation.co.uk

Chapter One

In the mountain village of Rio Lejos it was always assumed that Luis, the charcoal burner, would come to a bad end. It wasn't only his drunkenness that gave rise to this idea. After all, there were many drunken men in these poor villages of the western range who were respected rice farmers and citizens. It wasn't even his notorious cruelty, which sometimes erupted like a forest fire in the fag end of the long, dry summer, and resulted in the pain of many who stood, or appeared to stand, in his way. The notion had circulated since his birth, and had become as much a reflection of reality as the fact that donkeys can't dance, or that parrots, though they might speak of many things, can never mean what they say.

In the last long hour of afternoon, Luis came down from the mountain jungle that was his home, riding his donkey. He could be seen by the curious as he followed the winding trail to the river, emerging from the shade of the *bruscon* trees in the coffee groves to be silhouetted against the terraced cornfields in the slanted afternoon light. He was mounted well forward on the small beast, in front of a high load of charcoal sacks. His feet nearly dragged in the dust of the road. The donkey sagged under his weight as it struggled with trembling legs to avoid the rocks in the eroded roadbed. As the charcoal burner neared the shop, the donkey faltered momentarily, and Luis gave the animal a brutal chop to the side of the head.

Hector, the shopkeeper, winced. He was not a nervous man, but he had not risen to his present position in life by taking foolish risks. When he saw Luis dismount over the bent neck of the donkey, Hector felt automatically under the counter for his machete. It had never been used so far, but he kept it sharp and to hand as a kind of talisman. Usually, he would imagine striking some rowdy drunk with it, turned so that the flat edge landed first. He would shout at the same instant, and a combination of pain and awe would subdue the miscreant, or so it went in his occasional reverie. In the case of the charcoal burner, when he allowed his basically optimistic mind to dwell on the possibility, he struck with the sharp edge, and without warning.

Luis came in, holding two crusted bottles of wild honey in one large hand. His face, as always, bore an indecipherable expression which made him look like a distracted infant. It was streaked with the soot of his profession, and where the rivulets of sweat had eroded the ash, a complexion like cowhide was visible. He wore a sweat-stained fedora from which the brim had entirely rotted away, giving the impression of an Egyptian fez. He was shoeless, but his gnarled feet made the floorboards ring. He passed his eyes over the shop and Hector, finally fixing his gaze on the cage of the parrot Hector's wife had recently brought back from Las Aguitas. The parrot, an ordinary green bird of the forest, was chattering a combination of slogans, filth, and a cunning imitation of neighbourhood chickens.

"Good afternoon, Señor," Hector began blandly, caressing with his fingers the grooves of the machete. Luis put the bottles on the counter without answering the greeting.

"Two bottles of honey," he said curtly in a voice that was mossy with the jungle life he led, and too loud. "And three sacks of charcoal."

Hector wasted no time on preliminaries. "Three pesos for the honey," he opened, "and six for the charcoal." Luis squinted slightly, as if to make out the shopkeeper over a great distance.

"Three pesos for each bottle," he said flatly, "nine for the charcoal. And two bottles of rum from the top shelf."

"Twelve pesos for everything," Hector countered. "With one bottle of rum from the bottom shelf."

Luis did not answer. He let his eyes rest on the balding crest of Hector's head. There was a place there which began after some seconds to feel hot. Hector waited. He did not expect to win, only to present enough resistance to feed his pride, and to keep any future unreasonable demands to a minimum. He forced himself to stare back at Luis, at a spot where the dense eyebrows of the charcoal burner could be seen to just touch in the middle. He counted silently. He hoped his wife was listening at the door through which she had fled at the sight of Luis, and would later acknowledge his strength of character. At the count of thirty-five, he broke. As he opened his mouth to surrender, he was amazed to hear Luis say,

"Done. Twelve pesos, one bottle of rum from the bottom shelf. You will unload the sacks." His gaze left Hector's face dismissively and rested again on the parrot's cage. The bird had stirred and was looking intensely at Luis. As if on cue, it began a bawdy poem, one which Hector had observed that it never finished, and then lapsed into a series of wet kissing noises and an obscene suggestion.

"Very well, Señor," began a relieved Hector, "I'll..."

"And I'll have the parrot," said Luis, with an air of finality.

"But, Señor," pleaded Hector, trying not to whine, "you see, the bird is not mine. It, er, belongs to my daughter, who is, well, she is ill, you see..." His words trailed away as if even he had lost interest in them.

"The cage as well, of course," said the oblivious Luis. He inserted one oaken finger between the cage bars and waggled it at the parrot, who backed away. The decision was made. It wasn't that Luis had altered his bland expression so much as that there was a certain clearing away in Hector's mind of doubts about the extent of the charcoal seller's ruthlessness. Always practical, Hector ceased his speculation and began mentally to count his losses. Luis groped farther in the cage with his finger. The parrot squawked and retreated to the far side. The finger lunged, perhaps playfully. The bird screamed like a small girl. This amused Luis, who began to chuckle.

"Son of a bitch!" screeched the parrot. "Pig!" It was hanging stiff with fear from the top bars and glaring threateningly at the charcoal burner. Luis withdrew his hand, still chuckling. The expression on his face had shifted to that of a child drowning kittens.

"He is clever," said Luis. "Put him on the porch. When I return this evening, I will collect him." He watched while Hector stoically counted out the money and handed over a bottle of cheap rum. Luis twisted open the bottle with a quick wringing motion, grinning at the parrot, who was still glaring at him. As he turned away, the reedy voice croaked clearly, "So long, Faggot."

Luis spun and slammed one hamlike fist into the cage with such violence that it lifted from its hook in the ceiling and crashed to the floor at Hector's feet. Hector seized the machete handle with renewed strength. Luis said nothing but even the sound of his hoarse breathing was terrible. Gradually his rage diminished, like the passing of a squall, and his face resumed its blandness, which in some respects was even more frightening. He strode without comment to the door, but turned before leaving.

"Naturally, the bird doesn't understand what he is saying," Luis said calmly.

"Of course not, Señor," Hector replied, peeling his cramped fingers from the machete handle. "It is only an ignorant creature."

When the charcoal burner had gone, Hector's wife, Carmen, came into the shop from the back room. Hector sat quietly staring at the open door, wearing the graced expression of someone who has been robbed, but not beaten.

"Did you have to give that Devil my parrot?" she tried, but then something in her husband's face made her decide to shut up.

"Go and unload the charcoal, he said softly, and for once, without quarrel, she did.

Chapter Two

The charcoal burner's donkey stood on three legs in the moonlight, tethered to the porch rail. Except for an occasional shudder of the flesh at his shoulders, he was still. He was neither asleep nor awake, but wrapped in a familiar dream, which faded when he was driven or beaten, but returned when he was, as now, unneeded by Men.

A voice insinuated itself into this refuge. He twitched irritably and shifted his weight, but did not open his eyes. The voice came again:

"Are you awake?"

The question hung there, undeniably, but the donkey made no response. If he could not always understand, at least he could endure.

"Well?" insisted the voice.

"Don't know," muttered the donkey.

"What do you mean you don't know?"

"Don't know," repeated the donkey indifferently. There followed silence, but the donkey found himself unable to slip back into his dream. He resolutely kept his eyes shut, and made no move when he felt at last a faint pressure on his neck.

"Okay, let's go," the voice urged inexpertly.

The donkey rarely obeyed commands the first time, and so he did not change position. There was another faint tug at his rope. "I said, let's go!" the voice insisted.

"Can't go," said the donkey, "I'm tied up."

"Not now, you're not," said the voice, and the donkey opened his eyes a slit to see that his neck rope was indeed dangling free at his feet. Still he did not move. These events, though confusing, could perhaps be overcome by patience. He stood radiating silence, and there was no reply but the harmonies of frogs and insects in the night. He relaxed, and for this reason was shocked when the terrible voice of the charcoal burner seared his ears,

"Move, you lazy son of a bitch!"

The donkey spun away from the rail without thought, expecting a blow to the head. Wide-eyed he searched for the familiar squat figure, but saw nothing. Confused, he turned back to the rail.

"Not that way, you stupid sack of bones," the voice snarled. "To the road!"

He ran to the road, instinctively turning left toward the trail they had arrived by, but a curse and a surprisingly mild tug at his rope indicated a reverse. He turned quickly to the right and began a stiff trot through the darkened village. Still he could not see the charcoal burner, and the absence of his heavy weight on the donkey's back made his journey past the silent shacks of Rio Lejos seem unreal. But the fear of the charcoal burner was greater than his confusion, and he ran on, waiting as he went for the fall of the whip.

When this didn't come, and the last house of the village was well behind him, the donkey slackened his pace, at first experimentally, then with the doggedness of donkey habit. No blow fell, and he reduced the pace to a walk, then an amble. After a moment of this, he stopped, unconsciously flinching as he did, from the inevitable consequences of his defiance.

Nothing happened.

The donkey turned in a slow circle, searching for signs of the Man. Had he lost him somehow while trotting? That was unlikely, as the charcoal burner, even while drunk, was a tenacious rider. Besides, he had never actually felt him mount. Then had he imagined the Man's voice? Had he been dreaming? He rejected this idea at once, testing the night with its sounds and smells and finding it real and even ordinary, except for the fact that he was alone.

He swivelled his ears and opened his nostrils wide. There was nothing but the night around him. A cool breeze bringing rich smells from a distant barn, moonlight reflecting the shiny dark coffee leaves, and from a distance the perfunctory barking of a watchdog. There was nothing to explain how he found himself here without the charcoal burner. Ordinarily, on those rare occasions when he found himself temporarily free beside the road while the charcoal burner attended to some errand, the donkey would indulge himself in a short romp, or perhaps, a roll in the soothing dust. It had been a long time since he had had a roll, and even now, at this confusing moment, the impulse to roll free in the dust, crushing and smothering the tormenting ticks, was a temptation. He banished images of the charcoal burner from his mind and shifted his weight in the beginning of a soothing descent to the dust.

"Hey!" someone said suddenly, "Cut that out!" The donkey leapt involuntarily, eyes showing white all the way around. He peered wildly in all directions, but there was nothing to be seen.

"Who are you?" he cried out fearfully.

"Surely you realize," came the response.

"Are you..."

"Go on."

"Are you...God?"

"Of course I am. How clever of you to recognize Me."

The donkey struggled to consider this fact. The desire to sleep was suddenly almost overwhelming.

"What do you want?" he asked, straining to be seen as cooperative as possible.

"I want only your obedience, my child," replied the voice.

"And the charcoal burner?" the donkey dared to ask.

"Dead."

"What?"

"As a doornail."

"How do you know?"

The voice gathered force, and seemed to roar in the donkey's ear, "I know everything."

"But that's impossible," said the donkey without being able to help himself, "He's too..."

"Listen to me, my child," said the voice calmly. "I have been patient with you so far, but I will not put up with impertinence, do you understand?"

"Yes."

"Now I require you to walk for a while, until you reach the next village. There you will find a place to hide in the trees outside the place until morning. There I will contact you. Is that clear?"

"Yes, your, er, your honour," said the donkey.

"Very well. Go then, swiftly." The voice seemed to fade. The donkey stood in confusion for a moment and then turned and began an unaccustomed journey alone down the dark road. He was free, but he couldn't help the feeling that he would be happier with the drunken charcoal burner astride his back than with this burden of the unknown.

Chapter Three

Dawn surprised the donkey. He awoke on a patch of waste ground near a stream. He remembered travelling, but not arriving here, and was at once seized with a feeling of anxiety which he sensed could not be dealt with by flight, nor by kicking, nor even by, as a last resort, refusing to move.

On a branch of a nearby guava tree sat a parrot. He was peeling a guava fruit in his curved beak by rotating it with his tongue. The unbroken peel fell in a spiral halfway to the ground. He was watching the donkey coolly at the same time. The donkey felt moved to ignore him, and so began grazing the rough weeds unenthusiastically.

"Good morning, Ass," the parrot said, and before the donkey could respond, his voice roughened and became that of the charcoal burner. "I said, 'Good morning,' you evil-natured beast!" He growled convincingly.

The meaning of this occurred very slowly to the donkey, who finally looked accusingly at the parrot. "I see that you are not God at all, but only a parrot," he said.

"What do you mean, *only*? That's rich, coming from you."

"You tricked me," said the donkey bitterly.

"I think inspired is a better word."

"You made me believe I had to run away."

The parrot finished the guava fruit with a series of expert mouth operations. The peel fell to the ground.

"I suppose this means the charcoal burner isn't really dead, either?" asked the donkey querulously.

"How should I know?" said the parrot casually. He had returned to what the donkey supposed was his own, rather irksome voice.

"Now he will catch me," moaned the donkey. "He will use a stick to beat me, and I will die."

"Perhaps he won't. Catch you, that is."

"But he will. He is very fierce when he is angry," replied the donkey fatalistically.

The parrot pecked briefly at a louse on his wing and then ruffled all his feathers at once, so that he seemed suddenly larger, and bright glimpses of colour showed through the dull green.

"He will not catch you if..." the parrot paused maddeningly, "If you stay with me."

"What do you mean?"

"I mean that we shall escape him if you do as I tell you."

"You! What can you do?"

"I can outsmart him," the parrot continued calmly.

"What nonsense! No animal can outsmart a Man. They rule everything."

"Not me," said the parrot, with a brief flash of his yellow eye.

The donkey stared at him incredulously. He had never heard talk like this. He goaded the bird: "And where did you learn all this--this wisdom? Hanging in a cage in the homes of Men?"

It seemed to the donkey that the parrot gave him a pitying glance. He settled himself on the limb and began to talk in careful, condescending words.

"Long before your great-grandfather begat your line on some unfortunate mare I was within the homes of Men. By the time he died I was understanding their tongue and speaking it better than many." He paused, it seemed to the-donkey, for effect. The donkey feigned indifference by grazing at a few flower-topped weeds.

"I learned to entertain them, to make them laugh with obscenities which they never knew were parodies of their brutish lives. I was careful to conceal from them my understanding, for if they knew my contempt, or worse--my power--they would have killed me."

"I don't understand," said the donkey.

"No, you wouldn't."

"Why didn't you escape them, if you are so clever?" asked the donkey. "Couldn't you get out of their cages?"

"Bah!" snorted the parrot. "There was no cage I couldn't open when I was little more than a fledgling."

"Then, why--"

"Because the bastards clip my wings," the parrot snapped. He held out a wing, and the donkey could see the blunt edges left by the shears.

"But will they ever grow back?"

"Of course," the parrot said hurriedly. "It is only a matter of a few weeks. Days, really."

"But it doesn't matter, really," said the donkey. "Because there's no place to go, even if you can fly."

"There is," the parrot replied swiftly. "For those with the courage for the journey. That is why I will need your help."

"For what?"

"For the journey we must make," the parrot said. In his voice was not the slightest indication of doubt.

"What journey? Where is there to go?"

The parrot did not respond at once, but gazed over the trees into the sky. When he began to speak, his words had the sound of a refrain that he was reciting almost from memory.

"Ass, do you believe that there is a Valley where the green grass grows to your knees, where the rain falls, but never too hard or too often? Where the nights are warm and the days are cool? Where there are no ropes, no burdens, and no cages? Where--listen to me, Ass--there are no Men?" He hushed dramatically.

"No," said the donkey."

"No, what?"

"You asked me if I believe there is such a place. The answer is, 'no'."

"Then you are ignorant, even for a slave," snapped the parrot, sacrificing his detachment for the first time. "And you certainly don't deserve to go."

"Good," said the donkey. He walked away from the guava tree and began grazing deliberately. He cast an occasional glance at the parrot, who, exhibiting even more unconcern, had begun to peel another guava. In the distance the donkey could hear noises coming from the direction of the road as the world awoke. There was a particularly loud set of hoof beats, as if from a large horse.

"What's that?" the donkey asked nervously.

The parrot shrugged. "Perhaps that's the charcoal burner, on a borrowed horse. I'm sure he'll be following you, if only to enjoy your, er, consequences.

"What do you mean?"

"Well, didn't you say that he was fierce, and that he would beat you?"

"What shall I do?" the donkey nearly wailed.

"You have rejected my idea of a journey," said the parrot coolly. "I don't have any other advice, except, perhaps, prayer."

"But the journey is madness!" said the donkey. "There can be no place without Men!" The parrot shrugged.

"All right, then. Get on," said the donkey. "I will carry you."

"If you insist," said the parrot, and fluttered delicately onto the donkey's spine.

"Where to?" asked the donkey. "Which way?"

"Forward," said the parrot dryly. "And just hold it until we arrive."

The donkey resisted muttering. He began an easy pace but then, hearing fresh hoof beats from the road behind, launched himself along the stream bed at a nervous jog. He could not say what lay ahead, but behind him, like his own shadow, followed the wrath of the charcoal burner.

They travelled all morning beside the stream, along a path worn deeply into the hillside by the feet of other creatures. The donkey walked with his head down, not only to avoid the branches of the trail, but because he was accustomed to keeping his head as far as possible from the reach of his rider.

They skirted the village. Only once did they see any signs of Men. At the junction with a farm road they came upon a group of women washing clothes in the stream. They were slapping them handily against a large flat rock. Because the stream widened there, the donkey bent to drink, but the parrot hissed at him and dug in his claws.

"Not here, Ass," he whispered hoarsely. "Do you want to be captured?"

"But those women don't know anything."

The parrot said sarcastically, "How often do you think they see a parrot riding on a donkey? An untethered donkey at that, dragging his rope?"

"Yes, I see what you mean," said the donkey. He broke into a gallop as they passed the women, splashing water on both sides. One of the women cursed, then gaped in astonishment as they raced past.

"What was that all about?" said the parrot sarcastically when they resumed a normal pace.

"I thought it was better to get away."

"Just let me do the thinking from now on," the parrot said harshly. "You walk."

They continued along the trail in silence. The donkey stopped avoiding branches, as he sometimes did when the charcoal burner was dozing drunkenly on his back. He noted with satisfaction that the parrot was kept busy dodging foliage that might have swept him off his perch. He became hungry, but sulkily resolved not to let the parrot know.

They passed several choice grazing spots, where the long grass was at just that succulent stage before flowering, but the donkey plodded on. The sun reached zenith and passed on, leaving heat in its wake. The donkey's back was growing damp with sweat. From time to time the parrot shifted his position, but did not speak. Another hour passed, then two. They passed through a steep ravine, where other streams joined the main one and the water swelled audibly in volume. It was humid in the dappled shade, and the flies arrived from nowhere and sought the donkey's flesh. He found himself swinging his head rhythmically from side to side as he walked, to reduce the easy target his tender ears presented to the insects. When they finally cleared the ravine and found a flat, grassy clearing, the parrot spoke:

"All right, Ass. You can stop here for a while if you need to."

"Don't worry about me," said the donkey, thirsty and famished, but determined not to show weakness in front of the parrot.

"I think you should stop and rest," the parrot said reasonably. "You've got a long journey ahead of you."

The donkey stopped and began to graze delicately, taking only the sweet tops of the grass. He felt the parrot dismount and saw him hop into the tall grass toward a wild mango tree which had shed ripe fruits onto the ground. The parrot attacked the fruits hungrily, and the donkey felt a momentary satisfaction.

They ate and rested for an hour. The donkey cut a swath through the grass with his teeth that ended at the river. He put both forelegs in the water and bent and drank deeply. The parrot joined him, sitting on a rock and drinking with a series of bobbing motions. When he had finished, he mounted the donkey's neck and took his place on the ridge of coarse hair. They remained silent, but it was no longer the silence of contention. There seemed not much to say.

The donkey resumed walking along the trail, which now began to climb the hillside in a short series of switchbacks. They climbed into the slanting rays of the afternoon sun. At the top they found themselves on the ridge of a hill, which rose sharply past a coffee grove onto the high spine of a plateau. The sun was pleasant on the donkey's back after his rest, and he began to grow drowsy as he walked. The grip of the parrot's talons was becoming pleasant now, scratching his constantly itching hide. Suddenly the parrot hissed. The donkey came fully awake.

"What is it, Bird?" he asked, alarmed.

The parrot did not answer, but tightened his grip on his perch. The donkey turned his head but could see nothing except a hawk circling lazily overhead. But the parrot was riding hunched over, half buried under the donkey's ear.

"Is it the hawk?" he asked incredulously.

"Of course it's the bloody hawk," rasped the parrot. "He's been to-ing and fro-ing for miles now, damn him. Now I can tell he's seen me, because he just stopped overhead."

"But he can't hurt you, can he?"

"What do you mean, 'hurt me'? He could have me off your neck and eaten in five seconds, if only he knew it. It is a blessing that such a killer is also stupid."

"What should I do?"

"Go over to that coffee grove and walk between the trees. If he loses sight of me, he will probably tire of waiting and go away."

The donkey hurried over to the trees and pressed himself closely against them for cover. They were in shadow now, and the hawk could just be seen as he cleared small breaks in the foliage. After a few moments, he seemed to be gone.

The parrot preened himself as they left the shade of the grove, but looked carefully upward into the deepening blue of the sky before relaxing.

"In the Valley there is no problem with hawks," he said finally. "They need open spaces for their hunting. My place is in the jungle, where I can manoeuvre. Also, my colour protects me." His tone was defensive.

The donkey made no comment, and the parrot continued, growing reflective now that his danger had been avoided. "Of course, there are none of your kind in the Valley," he said. "You shouldn't mind about this, though. There's plenty of room.

"My ancestors are from here, you know. Not like Men, who came much later. Did you know that? We creatures are the rightful inhabitants of this place, not them." His voice darkened.

"When they came, they took everything that had been ours before, took it and burned it and cut it down. Many creatures died. Those that remain are still at risk. Men are evil."

"You don't have to convince me, Bird."

"No. Well, as I told you before, there are no Men in the Valley. It is cut off from the rest of the world by very steep mountains, too steep for their machines. It is possible to enter only by flying, or perhaps by a very sure-footed creature, such as yourself.

"On the other side is the sea, so, you see, Men cannot get in to spoil it." He scuttled animatedly up the donkey's spine.

"You will find it wonderful, Ass, even though..." he faltered.

"Even though, what?"

"I was, er, going to say... well, I don't know how you will take this, Ass, but it's the truth, nonetheless. Your kind are not from this place at all. Did you know? The Men brought you with them, as their slaves."

The donkey considered this, but did not respond.

"I'm sorry if I have shocked you, Ass." the parrot continued. "Of course it is possible that there is some land somewhere where you and your ancestors actually belong, but I'm afraid I have never heard of it."

"No," said the donkey. "I am sure there is nowhere where donkeys live that there are not also Men."

"I'm sorry," said the parrot. "I truly am."

Chapter Four

The sun was just above the tree tops when then the trail they had been following intersected a road. It was a pitted blacktop highway with deep gulleys on both sides. They had been descending throughout the afternoon toward an area of flat agricultural land, and the signs of Man had been increasing. Their trail appeared to cross the road, but it became an even fainter track that disappeared into a pine forest.

The donkey stopped at the roadside and nibbled a few stalks of grass while the parrot deliberated about which direction to take. There came the sound of a motor and the tooting of a horn.

"What's that?" asked the donkey nervously.

"It's one of their machines," the parrot said. "You'd better cross the road."

The donkey scrambled across the asphalt and continued along the narrow track toward the pines. When they were a few yards along, a pickup truck clattered by, carrying an overflowing cargo of people and goods. The noise of the truck spurred the donkey on, and he nearly galloped as they neared the trees.

"Slow down, Ass," the parrot hissed. "Listen!"

The donkey halted suddenly, shifting the parrot roughly forward on his neck. He heard it too, the unmistakable sound of excited dogs. Their barking panicked the donkey, who had been tormented by dogs before. He spun and began a dash back toward the blacktop road.

"Too late!" cried the parrot. Ahead, two dogs could be seen racing onto the track from a break in the pines. The donkey saw that they were cut off.

"What shall I do?" he moaned.

"Just keep going," the parrot said grimly. "We'll see if they're serious."

The donkey forced himself into a determined trot, but the dogs encircled his ankles and forced him to a standstill. They were a yellow puppy of considerable size, who was inappropriately wagging his scruffy tail even as he threatened, and an old dog of no particular colour who fixed his gaze on the donkey in a business-like way. He was clearly in charge. When the old dog saw that he had cornered the donkey, his barking changed pitch, and became the howl of a hunting dog over his prey.

"What do you want?" the parrot asked him shrilly. The dog turned slowly toward him in that exaggeratedly careful way dogs use to indicate barely restrained aggression.

"That is for you to explain," he said grimly.

"Yeah," said the yellow pup, perversely swinging his tail.

"We are just travelling through," said the parrot.

"I have never seen you around here before," said the dog, studying the parrot with slitted eyes.

"Of course not," said the parrot. "We are travellers, as I said."

"In fact," the dog went on, "I have never seen anything like you anywhere."

"Let us pass, and you will not see us again," said the parrot calmly, though the donkey could feel his claws tightening nervously on his neck ridge.

"That is for my master to decide," the dog growled. "My job is to watch and warn."

"Yeah," said the pup again.

"Warn of what? Two harmless creatures passing through?"

The dog scratched the soil stiffly with both back paws. He paused maddeningly and fixed the parrot with a yellow gaze before answering.

"I will tell you, stranger," he said carefully, "I am a dog of this place, a dog of no mean experience. In my years I have come to know what is right and what is not. I have come to recognize radicals when I see them. That is what you are, the pair of you. Radicals." He paused and glanced at the pup, who was studying him admiringly.

"Radicals," scoffed the parrot. "We are two creatures like yourself."

"What appears harmless can be very dangerous," said the dog sagely. "Very dangerous."

"That's right," said the pup.

The parrot sighed. "And if we decide to run?"

"Well," said the old dog, revealing yellow but useful looking teeth, "Then we will bite your jackass friend here until he cannot walk." The donkey started involuntarily at this news, bringing on a fresh spate of barking.

"Quickly, Ass," whispered the parrot into his ear, "See if you can get closer to that tree there." The donkey backed up until he felt the prick of pine needles at his flank. There was the sound of human cursing from the gap in the trees. At that moment he felt the parrot leave his back and scramble into the branches of the tree.

"Now go!" hissed the parrot, "Lead them away from the tree!"

The donkey moved forward a step, but was met with a furious round of growls and snapping charges at his ankles. A man emerged from the trees, carrying a shotgun and limping unsteadily in unlaced boots. The donkey felt hope drain away from him and stood limply in place. The dogs began a chorus of whining and tail wagging, but were cursed for their troubles by the Man, who lurched in the direction of the donkey and took hold of his rope. He said something rough and indecipherable to the donkey and hauled at the lead with great

40

force. The donkey planted his feet, more from fear than defiance.

"Go with him, Ass!" he heard the parrot rasp from the tree. "Don't worry!" As the parrot spoke, the dogs began a fresh fit of barking in their zeal to inform the Man of the bird's presence. He apparently hadn't noticed, and now turned his back and hauled mightily at the rope.

The donkey did not know what the parrot was planning, if anything. He knew only that he had been captured, and that the parrot was still free. He resisted the man's pull automatically, but his hopes sank. It seemed certain that the charcoal burner would get him now.

The dogs raged on, but the Man was oblivious to their complaints that the parrot was hidden in the tree. A donkey's length from the tree, the donkey heard a fluttering sound and felt the slight weight of the parrot as he mounted to his perch. The dogs' barking reached crescendo, forcing the Man to turn at last. He gaped openly as the parrot climbed coolly up the donkey's neck and peered at the Man through the donkey's ears.

"Polly want a cracker?" he crooned.

The Man laughed, exposing cracked and missing teeth. He extended a finger, urging the parrot to mount. The parrot hesitated coyly, then hopped gracefully onto the perch, warbling like a songbird as he did. The donkey thought he saw the parrot wink quickly at him. The Man began to pull again at the donkey's rope, holding the parrot aloft and cooing nonsense phrases at him. The donkey followed reluctantly, and the justified dogs jogged at his heels. He did not resist, and he felt nothing about the parrot's odd behaviour. He did not even wonder when a fleeting shadow passed on the earth beneath his feet and he looked up to see the hawk, circling patiently in the late afternoon sky.

He had been captured. Tethered to a castor bean tree near the Man's house, the donkey was despondent. He was within sight of the parrot, who was tied with a length of sisal string by one foot. He sat perched on the window sill of the kitchen building, a rough shelter of slatted palm boards. The shack was full of people, mostly children. From time to time they came out into the dark of the yard to look at the donkey. He did not acknowledge their presence, even when a large boy gave his ear an unexpectedly cruel twist.

The parrot, he could see, seemed to have settled in to his new captivity. He kept up a ceaseless patter of nonsense, causing much interest and laughter among the people. The donkey reflected grimly that it was all very well for the parrot to enjoy himself, as he would not be beaten senseless by the charcoal burner when he came. The donkey was certain, though he did not speak the human language, that the older son of the

Man had already been sent to notify the charcoal burner. It was therefore only a matter of time before the worst happened. The knowledge increased his bitterness toward the parrot.

He became aware of the presence of a creature nearby. Earlier there had been a few hens, now all gone to roost. They had not spoken to him, only muttered superstitiously to themselves. Now there was the sound of someone else, and the donkey turned and peered through the gloom behind him.

He saw a face, apparently disembodied in the darkness. Gradually he made out the rest of the form of a bird, like a chicken, but with oddly shaped feather patterns. He realized with some surprise that it was a cock, only he had been mutilated or barbered in a strange way. He was entirely bare of plumage halfway up his body, and the feathers that covered his back had been shaped into a ridge. His neck was a smooth as a fish. His head was left natural above his beak, but the contrast with the shorn areas made him resemble a pineapple. This threatened to make the donkey laugh, despite his circumstances, and he stifled a guffaw.

The cock continued his study of the donkey, cocking his head quickly left and right as if he were having to look around something in his way instead of peering through the wire of his cage. When he saw the donkey's attention on him he began a curious high-stepping strut across the front of his cage.

"Right," the cock screeched, "He's gotcha too. Gotcha tied up tight, damn right."

The donkey didn't respond.

"Got me too, got me in a box, got you tied up tight," he said democratically.

The donkey said, "Well, I know why he's got me, at least. Why are you in that cage?"

"Tomorrow's the fight," answered the cock. "Got me locked up tight, damn right."

"What fight?"

The cock inclined his head. "What fight? The big fight. All the cocks, damn right."

"What do you fight about?"

"About? About?" the cock was clearly confused. "They've got it coming. Kill them all. Damn right," he said vehemently.

"You enjoy it? Fighting others like yourself?"

"Not like me. Not strong like me. Look!" He drew himself up into a posture which made him look dangerously unbalanced and did a short promenade of the cage. "Damn right," he said.

The donkey was surprised to feel a familiar scratchy sensation on his shoulders and realized that the parrot had mounted unnoticed.

"Bird! What are you--" he gasped.

"Shhh! Do you want to get out of here or not?"

"Of course I do."

"Then be still and let me take care of it," the parrot said shortly. He hopped onto the donkey's forehead and swung agilely into the castor tree.

"How did you get away? You were tied up," the donkey whispered hoarsely.

The parrot paused on his branch. "Do you really think a loop of string can hold me?" he asked sarcastically.

"Then, can you untie me?"

"I already have," he said, and continued his course along the branch until he reached a clutch of ripened bean pods.

"Then let's go!" the donkey said, shifting eagerly.

"How far do you think we'd get with that collaborator, the dog, on duty? He'd have us in fifty paces."

"But we must go, Bird. The charcoal burner is coming, I know it," the donkey moaned.

"You're right, he is. Now just shut up and let me get on with it." He picked two large ripened pods and shook them gently so that they made a rustling noise. With a pleased expression he climbed back onto the donkey's head and scuttled rapidly along his back. He dismounted quickly. The donkey heard him hopping through the grass toward the kitchen. He wanted to call out, but did not dare. He watched anxiously until the parrot reappeared on his perch in the kitchen window. Incredibly, there was no sound from the people to indicate they had noticed his absence.

"Plenty stupid. Damn right," said the cock,

"What do you mean?" said the donkey crossly. "He may not look it, but that bird is a very intelligent creature. Look!" he said, and turned so that the loose rope hung free in the gloom. "He has already untied me."

"Damn stupid, all right. Big dog will bite you, farmer will put him in the pot."

The donkey saw the old dog come around the corner and glare at him suspiciously. He moved closer to the tree and let his head hang again as if he were tied. The dog went back into the kitchen and resumed his position near the bean pot, close enough to intoxicate himself with the rich smells of simmering pork fat, but not so near that the farmer's wife could hurl boiling water and abuse at him. The yellow pup, still inexpert, continually violated the invisible barrier, and was routinely scalded for his pains.

"Old dog, yellow dog," cackled the cock. They'll eat you up, damn right."

"Just wait and see," said the donkey defiantly, but he was feeling insecure all the same. The parrot had folded his head backwards under his wing, and seemed to be going to sleep. How could he sleep at a time like this? Was he mad? How were they going to escape from here? He tried to ignore the cock, who had resumed his arrogant promenade up and down the cage.

Ernesto was feeling very satisfied. Here he was, after all, with the family eating a good meal of beans and fat. Outside, securely tethered, was the donkey of Luis, the charcoal burner. He had recognized the crude brand on the donkey's flank at once. Earlier he had shared a laugh with the soldiers when they had told how the charcoal burner had returned from the whorehouse to find his donkey stolen or strayed, and, what is more, the parrot he had swindled from Hector the shopkeeper had flown the coop. Luis had been livid with rage, which he had demonstrated by kicking the posts of Hector's porch into the road, and then flinging the fallen sheet metal, piece by piece, into the forest. Hector, the soldiers said, had remained inside during this operation, only emerging after Luis had marched to the house of the taxi driver. Hector was carrying a machete, the soldiers said, a new one that apparently had never been used. But he had done nothing but stare at the damage before returning sadly inside.

The story had been entertainment enough, but then to have the donkey and the parrot turn up here this very afternoon! He had heard that Luis was offering a ten-peso reward for the donkey alone. As for the parrot, his son Ramon was under pains not to mention the bird to anyone. Ernesto thought he might enjoy having the bird himself. He was so full of sayings and songs that he could amuse them during the rains, when they were all confined to the shelter of the kitchen. And anyway, who would ever believe that the parrot would have stayed with the donkey?

Ernesto put down his empty plate and belched. He rolled a cigarette in a scrap of newspaper and smoked. The children were finishing their beans in the corners of the kitchen where they had taken their plates to eat alone, like little wolves. The old dog was begging now, and his wife obligingly slopped a mound of the beans onto a palm leaf. The yellow puppy moved forward to share, but one look of the old one's yellow teeth sent him cringing away. He whined softly beside the parrot.

Ernesto looked at the parrot. It was sleeping peacefully in the window. It had apparently gone outside a few moments earlier, but had returned and showed no sign of wanting to escape. Everything, it seemed, was going splendidly, and Ernesto fell into a contented doze.

He was awakened by a noise like a rusty hinge on a gate. He started, and came upright in his chair. The sound came again, this time accompanied by a whimper, and he was surprised to find that it had come from the old dog, who was lying on his side at Ernesto's feet. The noise came again, and the dog yelped. He dragged himself erect and began to stagger toward the door. Ernesto started to rise himself, then heard another, similar sound. He realized with a shock that this one came from his own abdomen. It was accompanied by a cramp so unexpected and so severe that he involuntarily invoked the protection of Our Lady. He went gingerly to the door and out into the dark in the direction of the outhouse. The pain increased, as did the urgency of his mission. He reached the toilet, only to find the door latched. There were unmistakable sounds of travail from within, a groaning which he was surprised to find harmonizing with one from his own throat. He rattled the door handle firmly.

"Marta, is that you?" he called.

He was answered by a groan which seemed to indicate assent.

"Can you hurry?" he asked piteously.

"No," came the response, though the single word contained several more syllables than was usual. Ernesto waddled despairingly toward the woodpile, but when he turned the corner was surprised to find two of his children engaged in the very act which Ernesto had in mind. He turned, feeling the will drain away from him, and fell to his knees. The pain was severe, but not as severe as the tragic realization that, for the first time in many long years, it no longer mattered if he reached the outhouse at all.

Chapter Five

The donkey came awake with a start to feel the claws of the parrot on his neck. Confused, he wheeled about, unconsciously looking for the charcoal burner. He saw nothing of the farmer or his family, or even of the old dog.

"Whoa!" the parrot cried. "Calm down and let's get out of here."

"But what about the Men?"

"Indisposed. They've got other worries at the moment."

"Where's the old dog?"

"He'll be that heap near the door," said the parrot cheerfully.

"Are they dead?" the donkey asked, wild-eyed.

"No, more's the pity," said the parrot. "And I'm sure they'd agree just about now." He climbed further up the donkey's neck and peered forward between his ears. "Now let's get this show on the road, Ass."

"Damn right," said a voice from the dark.

"The cock," said the donkey. "What about him, Bird?"

"What about him?" growled the parrot.

"Well, he's a prisoner, too, isn't he?" Don't you think we should help him escape?"

"Damn right," said the cock energetically.

The parrot did not respond immediately. The donkey thought he heard him sigh. At last he hopped forward, and quickly, almost distastefully, opened the cage.

"Okay, rooster," he said ironically, "You're free."

"Free, that's me," said the cock. He extended his head beyond the front of his cage and peered jerkily up and down, but made no move to leave it.

"Well, come on then," said the donkey impatiently. "Aren't you coming with us?" He caught the parrot's yellow eye, regarding him knowingly. He resumed his riding position on the donkey's neck.

"Let's go, Ass," he said.

"But the cock..."

"Can't you see he's not coming?" said the parrot abruptly.

"Come on, Cock," urged the donkey.

"Not tonight," said the cock. "Damn right."

The donkey stared at him unbelievingly.

"Tomorrow's the fight," said the cock defensively.

"Let's go, Ass," said the parrot harshly. He put his beak on the donkey's left ear, but did not quite nip it. The donkey turned reluctantly and moved slowly past the kitchen into the dark. There was no sign of movement inside, but he thought he could make out some huddled forms in the night as they rounded the corner. There was no sound other than a few soft groans. As they went up the narrow trail through the pines, the donkey thought he heard a plaintive "Damn right" from the cock.

At the junction with the road the yellow pup was waiting. He was standing broadside in their way, in imitation of the old dog's aggressive stance. As the donkey approached, cautiously, he snapped at them, "Hold it right there!" His adolescent bark was loud but unsteady. The donkey moved cautiously on, and the puppy suddenly retreated, yowling miserably. The donkey passed, and the young dog lunged suddenly at a rear leg. The donkey kicked automatically, and there was the sound of a hollow thump as a hoof connected with the puppy's ribs. The bark changed pitch and rapidly diminished as the puppy fled.

"That's the lesson for the day," said the parrot grimly. He was felt to relax his grip slightly, and the donkey resumed an easy pace toward the blacktop road. When they reached the margin of the pavement, he stopped, reluctant to put his hooves on the foreign surface, which even smelled faintly of Men. The parrot sat silently, and the donkey, after a second's hesitation, turned suddenly to his left and began a cautious walk down the extreme left shoulder of the road.

"How did you know the cock wouldn't come with us, Bird?" he asked after a while.

The parrot snorted. "What do you expect from a chicken? There are only two things a rooster likes, and the other one is fighting his fellow creatures for the amusement of Men."

"But you could have talked to him, Bird. You know how to explain things."

"What? And ruin one of Men's perfect successes?"

The donkey considered this. He did not understand the parrot at all. Even the effort it took to listen to him was almost too much. He plodded, seeking the semi-conscious rhythm that sustains donkeys when they are driven by Men, but thought began to trouble him.

"What did you do to the Men?" he asked

The parrot drew himself up with pleasure. "Ass, what you do when you are grazing and you come upon a castor bean pod?"

"I avoid it."

"Why?"

"Because it makes you sick," he said. "Does it make Men sick as well?"

"Ass, there are some areas in which even Men must suffer like the rest of us," said the parrot with satisfaction.

They travelled through the night. As the moon rose and crossed the mid heaven, the road surface widened and improved. Twice they saw the lights of cars, and each time the donkey leapt the ditch and hid among trees until they were past. He began to feel edgy as they approached the signs of Men.

"Bird, must we go through the city?" he asked nervously, as he had done several times before.

"Yes, Ass. I explained it to you already. If we try to avoid the city we must go the long way, through the mountain forests, where there are problems worse than Men."

"Worse than Men? What can be worse than Men?"

"What about jaguars?"

The word caused a ripple of fear down the length of the donkey's back. He had, it seemed, been born with a fear of these creatures, who, it was well known, prefer the flesh of donkeys to any other. He involuntarily quickened his pace.

"We will pass while Men are sleeping," said the parrot soothingly. "By first light we will be well past."

The road widened further. It acquired footpaths and curbs. Houses began to appear, and occasional cars sitting still but full of threat beside the road. There were poles stringing together lengths of wire. They seemed to the donkey to be leaning in unsafe ways, and he did not care to speculate as to their purpose. A few dogs could be heard, but they were jaded city beasts and did not stir as the donkey and his passenger hurried past. Still, the donkey's hide grew moist with the sweat born of fear. Even the parrot tightened his grip, as if the menace of the city might yank him from his perch.

They were passing alongside a row of rough wooden houses when the roar of the gun burst in their ears. It was a sound out of hell, which shattered the unsteady calm of their journey like a lightning bolt in a cloudless sky. The donkey went up on his hind legs, then scrambled with all four hooves for traction on the road. There was another blast, from a closer distance, and the donkey felt the hot wind as it blew past them. He began to run, tearing blindly along a board fence.

A sudden wrench on his rope yanked his head sideways and he wheeled about, nearly losing his footing. The parrot lost his grip, and the donkey felt him sail, flapping over his tail. His hooves clawed the gravelly pavement and held, and he found himself facing back the way he had come. Wide-eyed he saw the rope disappearing into a tough brown human hand. He responded by bolting, and the impulse was met with a massive tug on the other end. Another hand appeared and hauled the rope toward a shape now emerging from the gap in the fence.

A face appeared. It was a youngish Man, with dishevelled hair and an expression as wild as the donkey's. There was a shout, from another Man in the direction of the gunshots. The young man hissed and dragged himself forward. With the part of his mind that remained alert, the donkey could see that there was something wrong with this Man. As the Man threw his leg over the donkey's back, it was clear that there was only one. The other leg ended in a stump above the knee. A stick was heard to clatter to the ground.

The man lay flat across the donkey's back, and with one hand struck hard at his flank.

"Run, damn you!" he cried.

The donkey ran. Launching himself forward, he felt the sharp tug of the parrot's claws on his tail, but he did not hesitate. The parrot clambered up and gripped tightly as the donkey gathered speed. There were shouts from behind them, curses in a guttural voice and the screams of a woman. Then, so near together that they seemed a single sound, two more gunshots. The donkey felt hot pricking sensations, like horsefly bites, on his left flank. The Man on his back cried out in pain, but did not slacken his furious lashing of the donkey with the end of the rope. The donkey heard the parrot squawk distantly, and realized that the Man must be hitting him with the rope as well. Unable to think, he raced ahead, oblivious to the redoubled barking of dogs and the hoarse shouts of awakened Men.

He ran blindly, and even when the Man tried to slow his pace by hauling backward at the rope, the donkey's fear propelled him onward. When at last he slowed down, it was more from exhaustion than from the directions of the Man, who was doing little more than holding on. They had arrived in the heart of the city, surrounded by taller buildings of brick and many cars. There were confusing posts with lights on them, and a bewildering maze of connecting streets. In his insecurity the donkey gradually allowed the Man to take control. He sat erect on the donkey's back and gave him a few admonitory kicks.

He was driven down one of the side streets and began a descent down a long slope lined with rickety houses. The pavement ended, and gradually the street took on a more haggard appearance, with water-filled potholes and strewn rubbish on all sides. Another ten minutes brought them to a dirt road beside a high wire fence, behind which could be seen large buildings and a high chimney in the distance. The Man forced the donkey down the dirt road. On the side opposite the fence were a row of shacks made of rough boards and sheets of rusty metal. The Man hauled back painfully on the rope and dismounted with difficulty, clinging with one hand to the fence. With the other he tied the donkey's rope to the wire. He called out hoarsely. A light appeared in the nearest of the shacks. A woman emerged, carrying a candle cupped in her hand. She hurried to the fence, and when she saw the Man, she gasped. He leaned on her shoulder, cursing softly. Together they hobbled into the shack.

The donkey stood quivering. He seemed unable to get his breath, and so did not answer the parrot's solicitous queries. When he got hold of himself he became aware of the parrot perched on the wire beside him.

"Are you all right, Ass?"

"Don't know."

"The gun hit us. The Man had blood on his back."

"I think it hit me, too. My leg hurts."

"Just a minute," said the parrot, and disappeared. The donkey heard him in the grass at his feet and then felt a sharp biting sensation. He twitched but remained in place while the parrot worked. He felt the parrot's progress up his leg and along his spine.

"There were two stones in you from the gun, Ass. I took them out. I think you are all right."

"How can I be all right if I am captured again?" the donkey moaned.

"Don't worry about that. We shall escape again, easily."

"I am too tired to escape," the donkey said. "I have been captured twice today, and now I have been shot."

"Then rest," said the parrot soothingly. "At least we are far from the charcoal burner. We could spend tomorrow here, and escape after dark." He settled down on the ridge of the donkey's neck.

"At least I am free," he said. "The Man never saw I was there."

The donkey resisted a rude remark. He bent his head and saw a bit of grass growing through the fence with a few drops of dew forming on it. He nuzzled it with his lips, then opened his mouth to bite off a bit. He chewed slowly, and chewing, fell asleep.

Chapter Six

Dolores awoke before her husband. She lay for a while looking up at the palm thatch that was now beginning to show daylight through the worn spots. Beside her was the curled form of Epifanio. His hastily bandaged side was marked with small bloody spots caused by the shotgun pellets she had removed in the small hours of the morning. He slept fitfully, wiry muscles bunched rigidly. He had ground his teeth through the rest of the night, and more than once he had cried out. Dolores had slept hardly at all.

She got up carefully, insuring that her son Marco was not disturbed in his bed on the floor. Stepping over him, she studied she face that was so much like his father's, even to the worry lines he was acquiring at the age of six. Since her husband had lost his leg in the accident at the cane mill, the boy had become solemn, as if he knew that sooner or later he would become responsible for the family.

She went out into the covered bit of bare soil that served the family as a kitchen. In the dawn light she saw the donkey, standing dejectedly where he had been tethered the night before. One rear leg was raised, and she could see even at this distance that there were bloody patches in the hair near his flank. She splashed some water into a plastic basin from her five-gallon can and carried it out to the donkey. He started as she approached, and she could see at once that he had been beaten often. Though he was not old, he was showing signs of wear, and had become a little swaybacked from being overloaded.

Welcome, stranger, she thought. We are all swaybacked here.

The donkey drank greedily. When he had finished, Dolores moved his rope along the fence to a place where weeds were growing in abundance. The donkey looked at her briefly, and then bent to eat. She ran her hand gently down his back and over one raw flank. The flesh quivered as she stroked him. When she bent to retrieve the basin, the donkey followed her movements with one stoic eye. She went back to the kitchen to begin breakfast.

There was a little *yuca* left from yesterday, and some oil in the very bottom of the small jar she had borrowed from Conchita, her neighbour. By turning the jar upside down on her skillet, she extracted enough oil to cook the *yuca*. There was no milk. Perhaps she would get some coffee later when Conchita, who earned money as a prostitute, began to brew. She scraped together the unburned bits of wood from last night's fire and added some broken boxwood she had gathered yesterday outside the market. Using her last match but one, she resisted thinking of having to ask Conchita yet again for a light. If it were not for the boy, she thought, she would often go hungry rather than be forced to rely on her friends.

The fire came reluctantly to life. She laid the skillet on the flames, gently putting in the *yuca*, cut into thin strips. She squatted on her haunches and kept the smoke from her eyes with practiced movements of her feet and hands.

The smell of cooking food woke the boy. He came into view, rubbing sleepily at his eyes and holding himself at the crotch, as a child will do. He went to the fence to pee, and seemed not to notice the donkey until he had finished. He gave the beast a short glance and returned to the fire. It was clear that he was burning with curiosity-- Dolores could see the questions forming in his mind--but in line with his newly found adult attitudes, remained silent. It was just as well, she thought, because it spared her having to invent a way to explain the presence of the beast without revealing that

Epifanio had ridden him back from a chicken-stealing expedition. Perhaps the boy sensed it already. He gave her just the hint of a smile as she passed him a bowl of fried *yuca*, and ate it greedily with his fingers.

Dolores heard Conchita come out of her house and begin splitting firewood. Her ample arms could be seen over the thin hedge as they raised the axe rhythmically over the fat pine wood she had in plenty. Dolores, as always, tried not to be seen looking with envy. When one is forced into such close proximity with others, it is best to protect oneself with invisible screens. But Conchita was such a good-natured sort that it was difficult to remain aloof. Now that she had begun working as a whore, she seemed happier, or at least seemed to wish to convey that impression. Dolores let herself be seen by collecting some wood chips near the hedge.

"Hey, little friend!" Conchita greeted her. When she smiled, gaps in her teeth set off her otherwise handsome face. "Come and have some coffee with Conchita."

Dolores assented softly, indicating that her husband was still sleeping. The child had finished his breakfast, and without a word had shot off down the dirt road. He was leaving without a word these days, coming home later and later, sometimes bringing home scraps of food or clothing, occasionally a few coins. Dolores was afraid he was spending his time with the gang of young hoodlums who haunted the city dump.

She went around the hedge, carrying a piece of the *yuca* to share with Conchita. Her neighbour accepted it cheerfully, and popped it into her mouth as she bent to light her fire. When the flame was going well she balanced a pan of water on her metal grille and sat beside Dolores.

"Epifanio came home late last night," she said. It sounded like a question.

"Yes," said Dolores, studying the fire.

"But he was all right," Conchita continued.

Dolores shrugged. "I don't know what to say, Conchita. Since the accident, I just don't know what is going on with him." She stopped her voice from quavering, as it was inclined to do lately. "He is no worse than yesterday," she said, leaving out the shotgun wound.

She felt Conchita's hand on her knee. "Darling, have you given any thought to what Conchita has been asking you?"

Dolores sighed. It was too early in the morning to deal with such things. How could she tell Conchita that she would not join her working the bars without appearing to judge her friend? She let her silence answer.

"I see you are still not ready to face your situation." Conchita said with mock resignation. She poured boiling water through a nylon sock filled with last night's coffee grounds and left it to soak in the empty tin she used for a pot. The smell was wonderful, and Dolores forced herself to restrain her eagerness.

"It really isn't all that bad, you know," Conchita said casually. "You cannot pick and choose, it is true, but the average customer is no worse than a husband." Conchita's husband, a notorious drunk, had finally disappeared three months ago after threats against his life by Conchita's lover, now also departed.

"It is dark, you see," she went on. "Why, it could easily be my husband, except--" she laughed like a jack-o-lantern-- "They are usually much more gentle. And, of course, there is the money." She patted the cleavage showing above her soiled day dress, and Dolores imagined she could hear the rustling of notes deposited there.

"But, of course, for you--I mean, with Epifanio and all--I suppose it would be more difficult. Male pride is always impractical." She poured Dolores a tall glass of coffee. It was sweet with the brown sugar in which the beans had been roasted. Dolores sucked at the brimming surface. She noticed that her hands were trembling. They often shook when she tried to imagine this life of Conchita's.

"But I am making you unhappy, my darling," said Conchita softly, and put the clean back of her hand against Dolores' cheek. A tear had appeared there, but it quickly vanished. Conchita cleared her throat.

"I see you have acquired livestock," she said brightly, indicating the donkey.

"It is not ours," said Dolores.

"That's a question of interpretation, of course," Conchita said, grinning, "Possession is nine tenths of the law."

"He must have escaped from some farmer near here," Dolores said seriously. "No doubt he will be looking for his donkey."

Conchita studied Dolores' face. "My little one," she said softly, "I think you have not yet understood your predicament. Don't you realize that if things continue as they are, that you and your family will starve?" The last word hung in the air like smoke, and Dolores resisted an impulse to wave it away with her hand.

"I am no horse thief," she said firmly. "And neither is my husband."

"Surely this is not theft. A single donkey, overused at that, from the looks of him. A very small break for you."

"He is branded," said Dolores.

"That is easily remedied," said Conchita. She indicated the glowing edge of her cooking grille. "A single touch, that's all."

Dolores bit her lip. "I will pray about it. I will ask the Virgin for a sign."

"The Virgin!" Conchita snorted, not unkindly. "What does she know of donkeys?"

"She rode one, didn't she?" Conchita didn't respond. "I will ask her for help, as I do every day," said Dolores. "I still have faith."

"If you want my advice you'll sell that donkey and buy food for your child," Conchita said. She arose and began to pace. "Faith is fine, but you cannot serve it for supper. Whenever I pray to the Virgin, after asking forgiveness for selling my body to the cane cutters, I immediately ask her to send me even more customers. Even the poor must have help." She spoke animatedly, and Dolores began to worry that her voice would wake Epifanio. He must never know that Conchita was trying to enlist her as a prostitute.

"Listen to me, child, "Conchita said, "You must not be too good to accept what you are given. You do not even have that right. Do you understand?"

"Yes," said Dolores. She stood, aiming a weak smile at her neighbour. "I will wait one day, and then I will sell the donkey. If the Virgin does not wish it, then the owner will appear in time." She picked up the coffee glass, which was still half full and warm.

"Take my advice," said Conchita. "Tie that damned donkey tight."

"Yes," said Dolores, moving away.

"And brand his ass."

"Yes," Dolores said, and, under her breath, "If it is God's will."

She went around the hedge into her own yard. The fire was still smouldering, and she knelt and blew on it. She set the pan with the remaining *yuca* across it and went into the house.

Epifanio was awake, staring up at the thatch. He did not turn when she entered.

"Here is some coffee," she said cheerfully, offering the glass. He didn't move. She looked at the silhouette of his stump under the sheet. It twitched slightly, and she wondered if it was itching again. She set the glass beside the bed and went out again.

The donkey was dozing in the morning sun. As she approached she had the impression of something green suddenly flashing from his shoulder, but on second examination could see nothing. The donkey opened one eye and looked at her. She could read nothing in his expression. She put her hand to his neck and stroked the matted hair. She examined the knot of his rope. It seemed secure and not uncomfortable. The brand on his flank was three vertical bars crossed by a horizontal. She knew it would be very easy to alter. She touched the brand and uttered the name of the Virgin in the same instant, but no inspiration came to her. Only the echoes of Conchita's words and a cold feeling in her breast.

Chapter Seven

". . .Ass?"

The donkey did not answer the parrot, but twitched an ear to show that he could have if he wished.

"Are you awake, Ass?"

The donkey grunted. He had not spoken to the parrot all day, though he had watched him coming and going through the fence, keeping out of the sight of the people, harvesting wild fruits from the brambles that choked the wire. The donkey had eaten little, made uneasy by the cane mill and the Men who occupied it. His leg still hurt where the gun had hit him. He had stood still throughout the day, dozing and brooding. He was feeling sorry he had ever met the parrot.

"We should be off soon," the parrot said cheerfully. "The Men are sleeping now."

There was no sign of the people. The moon had risen above the forbidding silhouette of the cane mill, and the only sounds came from the night insects.

"Go yourself," said the donkey.

"What's that supposed to mean?"

"It means I am not going anywhere."

The parrot didn't answer, but shifted, it seemed to the donkey, fretfully on his perch.

"Do you want to know why?" the donkey said darkly.

"All right. Why?"

"Because I'm tired of being afraid all the time. I was better off with the charcoal burner." The parrot barely throttled a groan.

"Anyway," the donkey went ahead belligerently, "I don't think I believe in this Valley of yours." Unconsciously he planted his feet, as if hauling on his rope. "And besides..."

"Yes?"

"I don't trust you."

The parrot emitted a shrill cry of frustration. "What are you raving about?"

"You haven't been truthful with me," the donkey said truculently.

"God, this is rich," the parrot moaned. "Are you going to explain, or do I have to guess what you mean?"

"Don't play innocent, Bird. You were planning to leave me when the farmer caught us, weren't you?"

"But I didn't, did I? I stayed behind and helped you get away."

"Because you can't travel by yourself. And that's not all. I saw the hawk."

"What hawk?"

"You know very well what I mean. That same hawk. He's following us, isn't he?"

The parrot sighed. "Okay, Ass. Yes, he does seem to be sticking to us. But I don't understand why." He paused.

"And, yes, I do need you to travel. I never said I didn't."

"No. But you never said the charcoal burner was after you as well, did you?"

"What do you mean?"

"I've been thinking about it," said the donkey, "And it seems to me that you have been just as afraid of the charcoal burner as I am. Yesterday you said he would catch us when you were trying to get me to hurry."

"A manner of speaking."

"I don't believe you," the donkey said sullenly.

The parrot sighed loudly. He paced nervously on the donkey's spine.

"Let's get started, Ass," he pleaded. "I'll explain all this on the way."

"I'm not going unless you tell the truth."

"All right!" the parrot exploded. "If you must have everything explained to you, then just stand there and risk your freedom!

"Yes, the charcoal burner is after me as well. He bought me from the shopkeeper." His words were hard-edged with distaste. "That Man is the worst I've seen. He is violent enough to kill me for a wrong word. When I realized what had happened, I knew I had to act before he took me back to the mountains with him. So I joined up with you." The donkey shifted his weight, but did not interrupt.

"And, yes, you are right. I was going to stay free when the farmer caught us. But that was only so that I could rescue you more easily later. Really! But then I saw the hawk, hanging overhead, and I had to change plans."

The donkey didn't comment. He found he was enjoying the plaintive note in the parrot's voice.

"So you see, Ass, it is not what you thought," the parrot concluded. "And so now, if you feel better..."

"I'm not going," said the donkey.

"What?" the parrot nearly shrieked. He hopped off his perch and onto the fence, where he clung and hung extended toward the donkey like a gargoyle.

"You think you have found a good home, is that it?" he asked sarcastically. "Are you so content being the slave of Men that you take the first chance offered you to give up your freedom? You are no different than our friend the cock!"

"I am tired of being frightened," the donkey said defensively. "Anyway..."

"Anyway, what?"

"Well, that woman, you see. She gave me water."

" So?" the parrot sneered. "Even the charcoal burner gave you water, didn't he?"

"Yes, but she..."

"Go on, what did she do?"

"She stroked my back," said the donkey embarrassedly. "I think she is kind."

"I don't believe this!" the parrot croaked. He repeated mockingly, "She is kind."

"Yes," said the donkey defiantly. "I think she is."

The parrot drew himself up until he was inches from the donkey's face.

"Do you know what that kind woman is planning to do, Ass? She is going to get up in a few hours. After breakfast, she and that lame husband of hers are going to build up the fire until it is very hot. They are going to take a piece of iron and put the end of it in the fire until it glows red, then white." He paused dramatically.

"Then they are going to take the iron over to you-- her friend the donkey--and burn her mark into your stupid ass."

"You are lying," the donkey said miserably.

"Am I? I heard her tell the other woman. They are going to burn you and then sell you in the market."

"I don't believe you," the donkey said, but his voice dipped with uncertainty.

"Then just wait here, like the fool you are, until it's too late."

"But I thought...Bird, are you sure?"

"Why do you think I want to leave in such a hurry?"

The donkey stamped moodily at the ground, as if to erase the parrot's reasonable and terrible words. The parrot mounted quickly.

"I still don't trust you," the donkey said bitterly. "You are just out for yourself."

"Let me tell you something, Ass. Don't ever be surprised if creatures act in their own interests. In fact, you should worry if they don't. But in a choice, you must always trust them above Men, whose interests are always-- always--against the interest of the creatures." He shifted his weight forward.

The donkey felt his own will slipping away from him. The fog of uncertainty into which he had been plunged was so dense that it was simply easier to believe the parrot than to argue. He turned without enthusiasm from the fence and started up the dirt road. The moonlight now illuminated the rough contours of the house where the woman was sleeping. He glanced back once, wearily, before resuming his steps towards the parrot's dream.

They travelled slowly because of the donkey's sore leg and because he lacked enthusiasm. The parrot chattered to his companion in an unbroken stream, trying to speed his steps. They passed through a district of shacks. There was a sharp odour of sewage which burned the donkey's nostrils. The streets were strewn with litter, rotting garbage and things so old and soiled that even the poor would not have them. They saw no Men, and only the air of menace that the city itself exuded made the donkey keep up his pace.

He felt the claws of the parrot on his spine, and it seemed to burden him as much as the bulk of the charcoal burner. There must have been times, he thought, when the Man didn't require his services, when he was free to stand unmolested in the fields, to eat and dream as he wished. With the parrot there was never a time of peace, and the farther they now went from the proper place of donkeys, the worse it would undoubtedly grow.

Toward dawn they left the last houses behind and were again following a dirt road. The donkey kept his nose pointed in the direction of the rising sun, and the parrot made few corrections of his course. The elevation began to rise, and the donkey realized that they were already rising toward the mountains just visible in the distance.

When the sun rose finally, the donkey could see that they had skirted the city to the south, making a large loop around the places of Men. In reality they were still not far, despite the hours of walking. The donkey felt discouragement join his general mood of discontent. He stopped in the road and stood silently. The parrot hopped forward and bent his head over the donkey's brow.

"What is it, Ass?"

"I'm tired of walking. We've hardly gone any distance at all."

"Look, Ass, we're doing fine. Ahead of us are the mountains--can you see them? A few days, not more, and we'll climb them. On the other side is the Valley."

"When can I rest?"

"When we get to the Valley," said the parrot resolutely. Not until then. It's not safe."

The donkey grumbled, but started off again. He stayed in the high middle of the road, where the going though he knew the parrot preferred hugging the shoulder in case they had to escape suddenly. He found himself defying the will of the parrot in these small ways, just as he had sometimes done with the charcoal burner, despite the dangers.

The day grew warmer, then hot, as they climbed. The flies surrounded the donkey and seemed to concentrate on the raw spot where he had been wounded. He twitched his tail extravagantly, displaying his ill temper. His steps grew more grudging, and he stopped often to nibble grass despite the growing sense of displeasure of the parrot. He felt unfairly pushed by his rider, and it didn't matter to him whether it was the charcoal burner or this obsessed bird. The parrot, as if aware that further complaints would only increase the donkey's sullenness, clung stoically to his perch.

By afternoon they had reached an intersection with what appeared to be a new road. It was a well-graded expanse of soil with ditches on both sides. It seemed to head more directly toward the mountains, and the donkey turned onto it automatically.

"Hold it, Ass," the parrot said quickly. "I don't like this road."

"I like it," said the donkey. He kept up his dogged pace.

"There have been machines here recently. There are signs of Men all around us."

"There are Men everywhere," said the donkey acidly. He did not slow his pace, despite the nervous movements of the parrot on his spine.

"I tell you, there is danger ahead," the parrot said ominously. "We should stay to the small road, even if it takes us farther."

"It is not you who is doing the walking," said the donkey curtly.

The parrot did not reply, but tightened his grip on his perch. The road was a pleasure to walk down, and the donkey defiantly stayed in the precise middle. He sought and found a steady pace which was faster than they had been travelling earlier as if to support his position with the parrot, who remained nervously silent.

When they had travelled a mile, the donkey smelled something burning. It was a harsh odour not made by wood, and it made him nervous. But because of his defiant spirit he continued his pace. Ahead the road appeared to widen. As he drew nearer, however, the donkey saw that it in fact opened into a large clearing. What had seemed to be a hill could now be seen to be a huge heap of rubbish. Fires were smouldering in a dozen points along its crest. Unpleasant black threads of smoke rose into the sky, where hundreds of birds were swooping and circling. Hundreds more had landed and were sitting thick on the slope to their right. The other side was vacant, and the donkey automatically headed for that side.

"Hold it, Ass!" the parrot hissed. "There will be Men there!"

Confused, the donkey faltered. He opened his mouth to speak, but saw at once that the parrot was right. From over the crest of the hill appeared three ragged-looking boys. Their bodies were smeared with ash from their search for something useful in the refuse. One of them carried burden over his shoulder, a string that tumbled over his back and almost reached the ground. The parrot gasped. The donkey saw to his shock that it was a chain of birds, strung beak to tail like chilies drying on a town balcony. The tallest of the boys held the grisly string twisted in his fingers. He saw the donkey at the same instant, and gave a surprisingly hoarse shout. A second child reached for something at his belt, a forked stick with rubber straps dangling from them. The donkey did not know what the thing was, but a chill struck his heart at the same moment he heard the parrot cry:

"Run, Ass! Run like hell!"

The donkey wheeled about. As he turned he saw a second knot of boys appear at the other end of the rubbish heap. There were four of them, and they answered the tall boy's shout excitedly. Two of them raised stick objects like the other.

The donkey went immediately onto his hind legs, nearly dislodging the parrot, who began to shout instructions which were lost like leaves in the wind of the donkey's panic. He ran, and as he launched himself forward, he felt a sudden sharp blow to the foreleg. A second blow struck his forehead. They were under attack! He ran blindly forward, then realized he would trap himself against the rubbish mountain. He turned, and as he did, he heard a hollow thud as a missile struck something not himself. There was a flash of green as the parrot fell heavily to the ground. The donkey glimpsed him out of the corner of his eye, lying still in the dust with one wing limply extended. He raced ahead, driven by the shouts of the boys until he reached the edge of the trees. He was about to plunge into the undergrowth when he spotted a length of wire stapled to the trees. He wheeled about once again, and without any plan, found himself charging directly at the boys.

They scattered shouting as he ran through them. He veered again toward the trees and passed near the still form of the parrot. With one wild eye he saw the claw reach out and seize the dangling rope and hold on. The donkey found the edge of the clearing and crashed heedlessly into the trees, expecting to feel the ripping of barbed wire at his chest. Then he was through, tearing recklessly through the dappled light of the woods, dragging the parrot bouncing over the ground.

He didn't slow down until he reached a small stream, a trickle of water descending a slope. He turned and ran along its path until it cut deeply into the sides of the slope and became a ravine. When the open clay banks rose above the level of his back, he stopped and turned back to stare round-eyed at the direction from which he had fled. He had forgotten the parrot, and was surprised to see his small form lying at his feet. There was no movement except for a very slight heaving of the bird's chest to indicate that he lived.

The donkey strained his ears for sounds of the enemy. The voices of the boys could be heard very faintly. The donkey realized that he had run very far. He stood panting in the forest gloom until their voices faded. Still he stood motionless until a powerful thirst seized him, and he bent and drank deeply from the stream.

He seemed frozen in place. The sounds of the forest closed in as he stood uncomfortably motionless with two feet in the water. He was listening, straining as if to hear a familiar sound, but he knew there was nothing to be heard. It was more than an hour before he could bring himself to look again at the limp green bundle at his feet.

Chapter Eight

The sun set, and the donkey stood motionless beside the stream. Around him began the sounds of the night: frogs calling, the stream flowing, the rough wheeze of his own breath. There was no sound from the parrot, who was lying tumbled out on the bank like something spilled from a basket. The donkey found he could not look at him. He was caught, he realized. Just as the comfort of his Dream now eluded him, the prospect of planning and thinking and trying was beyond his reach. He could sense the contours of this new life, but he could not grasp it. The parrot, who seemed to relish uncertainty, could explain things to him. Even if they did not make sense, at least it was possible to believe that the parrot himself understood.

The donkey shook himself. The parrot, he realized, might die. He must now try to consider where he was going. He made an effort, but all that came was the figure of the charcoal burner creeping up behind him with a large stick. He thrust the image aside and tried to concentrate on the road ahead, but the way seemed even blacker than the darkness here by the stream. Where could he go now? He could not remain here, in this bramble patch. There had been that place, the woman who had stroked his side, but the parrot had said she only wanted to sell him. That was back, and somehow he felt that his path lay forward.

The Valley, said the parrot, lay over the mountains, perhaps these very mountains that began here and ran eastward toward the sea. There was grass there, the parrot had said, and no Men. The donkey fought off despair at the thought that the parrot was mad. There could be no place where Men had not come to rule over animals. The Valley could not exist, as the parrot claimed. There would be a mountain, and then Men and another mountain, and more Men. And in between, jaguars. The word made the coarse ridge at his neck rise. His back felt open to the darkness. The trees enclosed, trapped him. Were there jaguars here? He moved nervously, disturbing stones, which splashed into the stream. The sound made him wheel about. The night was full of jaguars and Men, and it would always be so. There was no safe place for him: no Valley, no kind owner, not even the Dream. He forced himself to steady, to put all four hooves on the ground and to wait. The cold touch of panic began to leave him and, as it did, it left in its wake weariness and, without meaning to, the donkey slept.

When he awoke, the moon had slipped overhead, and now cast nearly vertical pale light into the ravine. The trees had not lost their sense of threat but now seemed to shelter him. He looked for the body of the parrot but was surprised to see it was gone. His first thought was that some animal had taken him while he slept, but then a sudden hope that he had recovered. He turned abruptly, looking for signs of the parrot's departure.

"Hey!" said a weakened but familiar voice, "Hold on a minute! Are you trying to throw me off?"

"Bird! How did you get up there? I thought you were, you know. . ."

"Dead. I will be if you don't calm down a bit."

"Are you all right? That stone hit you very hard, I heard it."

"So did I," said the parrot wryly.

"Can you travel?"

The parrot didn't answer. His breathing could be heard, shallow and wispy, like dry leaves rustling. His grip on the donkey's nape was sharp, but somehow tenuous. The donkey moved cautiously downstream a few paces toward a dense bramble bush which was all but covering a few stalks of sour grass.

"We can't stay here," the donkey grumbled. "There is nothing good to eat." The parrot remained silent, as if hoarding his strength. The donkey grazed desultorily.

"Bird," he couldn't help asking, "What were the boys doing there, on the rubbish mountain?"

"They were killing," came the terse reply.

"But why? Are they going to eat all those birds?"

"Some of them will be eaten. The rest were merely killed for sport."

"But then there is no need for them to do it."

"That has never stopped Men from doing things like that to creatures."

The donkey considered this. "Perhaps there is some reason we do not understand," he said hopefully. "It cannot be that Men are all mad."

"They are not mad, Ass. They are simply arrogant. The parrot coughed. "I could tell you things that would make you lose hope."

"But they suffer, Bird. Those boys, they looked dirty and sort of sick."

"Yes, they suffer. Those boys have no proper food. They are beaten by their parents. They spend all day sorting through the garbage of others to find something useful to eat or sell. You might suppose this would make them sympathetic to the suffering of others." He laughed dryly, and the laughter became a cough.

"So the charcoal burner, Bird--he is not mad?"

The parrot made a harsh sound like barking. "Sometimes Men are also mad," he said.

Morning caught the donkey by surprise. The dense wood in which they had taken refuge kept the sun's light from them until a ray burst upon the donkey's eye through a gap in the trees. The parrot appeared to be sleeping, with his head tucked under a wing. In the daylight the donkey could see a mottled patch where blood had dried on his breast. The small chest rose and fell rapidly. It occurred to the donkey that the parrot had been more badly injured than he cared to admit.

He went a few paces upstream, away from the thicket of brambles, and drank. Though it was early, the air in the ravine was still and unpleasantly humid. Gnats were already pricking his ears. He swished his tail involuntarily and saw that he had awoken the parrot.

"Good morning, Ass," he said almost cheerfully. He made his familiar transit up to the donkey's head. His grip seemed stronger but his movements were painfully slow.

"Could you bend down a bit?" he asked casually. The donkey lowered his head to the ground without comment, and the parrot descended carefully to the ground. The donkey thought that if the parrot needed this help, he must still be very ill. The parrot inched his way to the stream and drank, bracing one wing against a stone. He finished and folded his wings carefully around him like a blanket.

"You know, Ass," he said, "I think it might be a good idea if we stopped here for a day or two, until you've got your strength back. You look a bit peaked, you know. After all, you were shot by the gun. He paused for breath.

"Here? What about the mad boys?"

"They are on the other side of the hill," the parrot said. "Anyway, they won't dare come into the forest."

The donkey started to protest, but felt the urge slip away. The parrot's will, even when he was injured, was too strong to fight without good reason. He sighed. The parrot slowly remounted and promptly went to sleep again. The donkey grazed dejectedly in the sour grass by the stream.

All day, while the donkey grazed and nodded in the stifling air of the ravine, the parrot slept. As the donkey shifted position he bobbed senselessly, but held his grip. Once he called out in a voice the donkey had not heard before, a pure sweet chain of syllables that fluted liquidly in the silence. The donkey thought that perhaps this was the true voice of the parrot, when he was neither imitating Men nor talking to other creatures. It was a joyous voice from the morning of the world, and despite himself the donkey began to hope.

At dusk the parrot stirred, and dismounted without speaking, to drink. He returned laboriously to his perch and slept again at once, leaving the donkey feeling somewhat frustrated. He could not seem to sleep. The gnats had had their fill of him all day, and now he stood wide awake and itching in the gloom. The moon rose again and shed anaemic light into the gorge. There were shadows which seemed to the donkey's eye to resemble large stones and clear pools and patches of sweet grass. Some appeared to move as he shifted his gaze, racing out of his sight like living things. He did not really think they were animals, but found himself unable to ignore them. They became faster, larger, stealthier. They lost their tenuous quality and began to demand recognition. He found his thoughts avoiding the thought of--there it was--jaguars. Of these he knew little, except that they seemed to prefer the flesh of donkeys to all other creatures. An image formed itself in his mind of a larger version of the semi-wild orange cat who appeared from time to time at the home of the charcoal burner. This had been a particularly uncommunicative creature who hunted mice by the barn and then ate them a leg at a time while they tried, increasingly less successfully, to escape. A jaguar would be bigger, thought the donkey, feeling a shudder creep up his spine, perhaps so large that they could eat a donkey in the same way. It was not impossible. It seemed to him that since he had begun this journey with the parrot, anything at all had become possible.

Self-pity mingled with his growing fear. If a jaguar came, would the parrot be able to help? Would he even try? Jaguars would have no interest in parrots, and so they would not fear them. Could the parrot deliberately lead the donkey into danger? He moved restlessly. "Bird?" he whispered. "Are you awake?"

"I am now," said the parrot crossly. "What is it?"

"Nothing, really."

"Come on, Ass. Out with it."

"Well, I was just wondering. About, er, jaguars."

"What about jaguars?"

"Well, if there were any, you know, near here."

"I see," said the parrot. "Got the night creeps, have we?"

"What's that?"

"You see that tree over there?" asked the parrot, painfully inching his way up the donkey's neck. "The one with the vine growing around it? That part about head height that's sticking out a bit. That looks a bit like a paw, doesn't it, a large paw?"

"A little, maybe."

"And up higher, there, where it's thicker--why, that could be a head, you know? A really big one. And when the wind moves it a little--like that, see? It looks almost alive. In fact, it looks like a jaguar! Yes, a giant jaguar, ready to pounce and rip your flesh!"

"Cut it out, Bird!"

The parrot made a disparaging croak and descended again to his favourite perch on the donkey's shoulder.

"Shadows, Ass. Nothing real. There are no jaguars here. They like Men even less than you do, because Men kill them on sight and make rugs out of them."

"Then where are they? They must live where there are no Men. Somewhere like the Valley!"

The parrot did not respond at once. His silence confirmed the donkey's fears. Of course! The parrot was leading him into danger, not away from it. When the parrot finally spoke, it was in a calm, low voice, though whether it was designed to quiet the donkey's fears or due to his injury was not clear.

"You are being foolish, Ass. First, scaring yourself with these night shadows and then inventing more shadows in your mind. I have told you that there will be no problem with jaguars in the Valley, nor with Men."

"But how can I know?" the donkey wailed.

"You must trust me," said the parrot, in a way that indicated he was finished with the conversation. He turned his head backwards significantly and appeared to sleep.

In the morning the parrot was much improved. He lowered himself to the ground without asking aid from the donkey, and stood unsupported to drink from the stream. The donkey noted with mixed feelings that the parrot was going to live. He watched as the parrot plucked an immature fruit from the bramble bush and ate it delicately. When he had finished, the parrot fixed him with a bright eye and said,

"Well, Ass. I must say you are looking better today. A little rest was exactly what you needed after all.

"But I--" the donkey began.

"And after that bit of foolishness in the night about the jaguars and all that, why you seem a new ass."

The donkey found himself mute.

"We shouldn't dawdle here, though," the parrot said, picking another berry. "We are not so very far from the Valley here. A matter of days. Along these mountains here, over the top, and we're there." He mounted with rising agility. "So, if you are ready. . ."

The donkey found himself moving automatically, propelled by the faith, or the madness, of his passenger. He turned uphill and they began to climb a long slope that rose easily alongside the stream. He could not see his path. Beyond the few steps in front of him, but by now that had ceased to be important.

Chapter Nine

They travelled steadily, but without haste along the lower slope of the mountains, avoiding the places of Men, but not entering the deep forest. The parrot improved rapidly. When they passed a tree in fruit, the donkey would stand beside it while the parrot climbed up into its branches to eat. The parrot began to groom the donkey's sore ears, ferreting out the ticks and mites which had caused the donkey suffering for so long he had forgotten what it felt like not to hurt and itch. The parrot told stories of how the world was before Men came, and gradually the donkey forgot his worries and yielded to the fine days in the dappled shade of the wood.

One morning they happened accidentally upon an open place in the trees which had been burned. The soil was black and still hot under the donkey's hooves. The acrid smell disturbed him with its impressions of Men. They retreated and gave the clearing a wide berth.

"It was Men who burned that place, wasn't it?" the donkey asked.

"Who else?" answered the parrot grimly.

"Why did they do it?"

"They wish to grow their beans here. The forest soil is very good."

"Surely there are better places for beans." said the donkey, a little provocatively. He had begun to enjoy goading the parrot into speeches about Men.

"The better places are all taken. The ones who burn the trees are the poor who have no land."

"Then one day they will burn it all."

"Exactly. That is their destiny."

"I cannot believe even Men wish to destroy the world."

"They do not wish to destroy the world exactly," the parrot laughed hoarsely. "They wish to destroy each other by taking all the good land for themselves."

The donkey considered. "But even animals do that, don't they? Compete with one another?"

"Creatures compete, yes. A creature is a self-interested being. But it will never take more than it needs, and it never kills for pleasure. That is the speciality of Men."

They stopped at a pool to drink. The afternoon was bright, and the sun shone down on them through a clearing in the trees. The donkey gazed absently at the dragon flies trawling the water. The parrot waded lazily in the shallows, hunting fat flies. There was no sound except that of the insects. The donkey let his mind wander. He felt rather than saw the shadow when it passed over him. Still too somnolent to raise his head, he searched the reflecting surface of the pool and saw a familiar figure turning lazily overhead against the blue. It was the hawk. He started to speak to the parrot, but his companion noticed the hawk as the same instant. He hopped rapidly into the shadow cast by the donkey's body and stood still.

The donkey watched the hawk. It was watching them, unmistakably, turning in tight orbits which kept him in the line of sight above the trees. Its spread wing feathers and the red plumage of his tail were clearly visible, even to the donkey's less acute eye, so how much more closely was he observing them?

"It is the same one, Bird," said the donkey.

"Don't you think I know it?" the parrot nearly screeched. "It wants to make a meal of me, can't you see?" He grabbed the rope with his beak and began rapidly climbing.

"Let's get out of here. Go into the dense part, under the trees."

The donkey complied, and sought a particularly dark patch near a wild mango tree. The parrot paced anxiously on his pine and peered constantly upward. The hawk could not be seen.

"Perhaps we've lost him," said the donkey lamely.

"You don't lose a hawk that easily. This one has it in for me, all right. I can't understand it." He continued to pass and peer. The donkey waited restlessly.

"It's no use staying here until dark," the parrot said. "He'll just wait up there. We must go into the forest now and start up the mountain."

The donkey shifted nervously. "I don't want to go into the forest now," he said truculently.

"We're going," said the parrot grimly.

"There are jaguars in the forest. You said so."

The parrot let out a long sigh. He seemed to be counting.

"Look, Ass," he said in a more conciliatory tone, "If we are going to reach the Valley, we must climb sometime. It might as well be now."

The donkey planted his feet. The parrot ascended to his head and hung down over the donkey's forehead. He looked impassively into the donkey's stubborn face for a moment before saying,

"Do you really think I'd lead you into danger, Ass?" he said soothingly.

"It's all very well for you. Jaguars are not interested in parrots."

"So we should remain here, where the hawk is," said the parrot. "Is that fair?"

The donkey wavered slightly and indicated it by shifting his weight slightly.

"If you do as I tell you," said the parrot seriously, "I will protect you."

"From Jaguars?"

"From Jaguars."

The claim was made in such a reasonable tone of voice that the donkey felt himself half believing it. He tried to frame a rejoinder, to scoff at the parrot's words, but found that he wished to believe. After a further hesitation, made more from pride than conviction, the donkey turned in the direction of the slope. The parrot settled into his riding posture, and not a word was said of the hawk, or the parrot's victory.

Chapter Ten

The donkey climbed. Upward through the dense brush he ploughed forward, impatient now to arrive somewhere, even if it meant disaster. The parrot clung tightly to his nape to avoid being swept off by branches, and spoke little.

Night fell, and the humid gloom of the forest was replaced by nearly total darkness. The donkey moved more by feel than by sight, but his path was always upward. The air cooled and the sweat dried on his back. His breathing was the only sound either of them could hear apart from the yielding of branches. He grew thirsty but ignored it, and still he climbed.

Toward midnight they reached a stony mountain face where the trees cleared, and for the first time the donkey could see the stars. There was the sound of water trickling over stones, and after a brief search the parrot found a thin stream emerging from a crack in the rock. They drank gratefully, and the donkey lapped at the wet stones with his tongue even after he was satisfied. His muscles quivered with fatigue. Despite his impatience, the parrot said nothing, even when the donkey faded gently into sleep.

He awoke suddenly, aware that the coarse hair on his back was standing erect. The parrot was a few yards away, perched silently, and it seemed, forebodingly, on a rock. There was something amiss, a sense of not-quite-rightness so subtle that the donkey was not even sure how he knew it. Was there a scent? Indistinct, sweetish and yet acrid, it did not quite reach the threshold of awareness, yet had the power to seize the donkey with a leaden grip.

The parrot seemed agitated. When he saw that the donkey had opened his eyes, he left his perch on the rock and hopped onto the trail.

"Stay here, Ass." he said, and turned toward the slope.

"Where are you going?" the donkey asked, holding panic at bay with artificial calmness.

"Relax. I'm just going up here a way to have a look." His yellow eye was steady but unsmiling.

"Is there something..."

"Be calm, Ass. I'll be back in two shakes." He turned and hopped surprisingly spryly into the brush.

The donkey stood unmoving. He had the feeling it would be better if he remained this way, as solid and silent as a stone. His mind, too, must be still, and ignore the panic that threatened to enter, to overwhelm him and send him galloping blindly down the mountain. He could not consider what might happen if the parrot failed to return and if his promise of protection had been only more words. Eyes shut, head down, he waited.

The parrot climbed haltingly up the slope. He had skirted the stone face on a small rocky trail which rose steeply to a terraced open area above the rocks. He found a dead tree encircled by a parasitic vine and climbed, beak over claw into the highest branches. He nestled himself securely into the covering leaves and looked down upon the large jaguar waiting below.

The big cat was semi-crouched at the edge of the terrace, his head and paws over the edge in the direction of the stone face and the donkey. He was rippling his muscles luxuriously in self-enjoyment and anticipation of a good meal. The parrot rustled the leaves of his perch and the big head swung around, showing green eyes that seemed to be lit from within.

"Who's that?" he growled.

"Who, indeed."

"Oh, it's you, Owl. Be quiet, will you? I'm trying to hunt."

"What are you hunting?" the parrot asked owlishly.

'Not that it concerns you, but there's a fine hunk of donkey meat coming this way that's just begging to be eaten."

The parrot made no comment, but produced owl-like reflective sounds. The jaguar yawned pointedly.

"So if you don't mind, Owl..."

"I never interrupt a fool in his folly."

"What's that supposed to mean? Don't bother me with your wise guy act." he snapped.

"Wisdom consists in understanding what one sees," said the parrot.

The jaguar turned his powerful body toward the tree and let his tail flick menacingly. "You want to explain that?"

"Tell me, Jaguar, what is a donkey doing here, halfway up this mountain in the dark?"

"Well," said the jaguar reluctantly, "Maybe he got lost or something. Who knows? Maybe his master left him for some reason."

"Maybe he flew," said the parrot drily. "And maybe you'll like being a rug on some hunter's hearth!"

The jaguar showed his teeth reflexively.

"That donkey was left there on purpose," said the parrot relentlessly. "He is bait, in a jaguar trap. Have you not noticed the rope on his neck? Where there is a donkey, there is a master. And his is surely waiting for an unwise jaguar, waiting with guns."

"That's stupid," said the jaguar uncertainly. "I never heard of anything like that."

"Probably the last jaguar who did is decorating a Man's fireside even now. Another jaguar who allowed himself to think with his stomach."

"You're making me mad, Owl," said the jaguar. Why don't you go catch a mouse or something?" He showed his teeth again, but was crouching less serenely, with one eye on the trail below.

"I was just thinking how the Men would not necessarily wait for a jaguar to attack. It would be better to find him while he was still stalking. That way they could use the same bait again, for another fool."

"You're asking for it!" snarled the jaguar, rising to his feet. He moved toward the tree confusedly. The parrot didn't answer, but there came, from an uncertain direction, the distant sound of voices, as if carried on the wind. The jaguar spun about, ears erect.

"What's that?" he hissed, poised to run.

The sounds increased in volume and became hoarse voices, rustling brush and twigs cracking underfoot, metallic clicks.

"Sounds like Men," said the parrot mildly, but the jaguar was no longer there. A slight disturbance of the undergrowth was all that marked his instant departure.

"Very wise," said the parrot in one of the Men's voices," for a fool."

The donkey heard the parrot's approach and opened his eyes a slit. His companion swung onto his perch jauntily.

"Is it all right, Bird?" asked the donkey.

"Yes, Ass, everything's fine."

"Then there was no..."

"Jaguar?" interrupted the parrot. "What gave you that idea?"

"I thought I smelled something then. I don't know."

"I told you, Ass." said the parrot breezily. "You must learn to trust me." He settled himself for the trek. "Jaguars, indeed," he said.

Chapter Eleven

They climbed through the night, not even pausing when the sun broke through the forest cover and once again brought swarms of stinging gnats. They spoke little. The donkey needed all his breath for the climb, and the parrot, perhaps afraid that speech would interrupt their progress, merely leaned into their path without a word.

Once they stopped for water at a tiny spring. The parrot ate a few green grass shoots, but the donkey stood silently with shut eyes until they began their uphill trek again. At some point along their way the donkey must have fallen asleep, because toward sundown he was awakened by the parrot's movements along his spine.

"Where are we, Bird?" he heard himself asking through dry lips.

"We are only a few hours from the top, Ass," the parrot answered excitedly. "From there we will be able to see the Valley."

The sound of the word had a curious effect on the donkey. It seemed to have acquired a different and more urgent ring as they neared their destination. Because he couldn't imagine such a place, it was as if he expected the parrot to reveal more doubts about its existence as he was closer to having to show his dream. Instead, the parrot's eagerness was reaching fever pitch, and the Valley was beginning, even to the donkey, to sound possible. "Can you go on, Ass? We could probably reach the summit if we tried hard."

For his answer, the donkey merely turned and headed automatically up the slope. The parrot resumed his vigilant posture peering over the donkey's head, dodging branches when necessary. They climbed through the waning afternoon light until the trees began to thin and yield to

131

rough shrubs and grass. The way became increasingly stony, and several times the donkey lost his footing briefly. Once they went around a large stone outcropping, only to find that their way was blocked by a deep ravine on one side and a stone face on the other. The donkey retraced his steps patiently, but found the descent more difficult. When it became too dark to make out the surface of the ground ahead, he slowed and finally stopped.

The parrot exhaled, a long sigh of disappointment. He dismounted quickly and found a perch on a branch beside the donkey, who stood for a while without moving.

"It's a matter of a few minutes now, Ass," the parrot said. "It's too dark now, but we'll certainly make it in the morning…"

The donkey merely grunted. He was too tired to open his eyes. He realized he should eat something, even this rough grass of the rocky slope would give him strength, but he could not. I will rest for an hour, he thought.

He awoke to feel the parrot apparently tugging at his rope. He shrugged irritably, but the tugs continued. He opened one eye and saw the parrot working with his beak at the knot, which had grown so tight that it was almost fused into the rope. The parrot worked until he freed one loop, and then the rope fell quickly to the ground.

"There," said the parrot with satisfaction.

The donkey's neck felt suddenly lighter, even though the rope weighed very little. He looked at the coil of rope at his feet and then pawed it with one hoof, finally kicking it away into the darkness.

"You won't need that now," said the parrot solemnly. "You will never wear a rope again."

"I cannot remember when it was put there," said the donkey. It must have been the charcoal burner, but I can't remember. Isn't that strange?"

"Not so strange, Ass. With luck you will forget all about the charcoal burner in the Valley."

"It feels odd, though, Bird. My neck feels lighter."

"That's freedom," said the parrot. "Wait until you see the Valley."

The donkey tried to imagine the Valley, but as always, found he could not. He was content with the sound of the word, and the confident note in the parrot's voice. Drowsiness overcame him, but as he went under, a thought occurred to him. He considered it, but found he could not fathom the idea alone. "Bird, are you awake?" he asked timidly.

"Yes," said the parrot, and the donkey could tell that he had been waiting.

"If I'm free now, who do I belong to?"

The parrot hesitated just a second.

"Nobody," he said. "You are nobody's ass."

The sun woke him with a full beam of light shining directly into his eyes. He was startled to see that he had slept well past dawn. He was surrounded by chest-high brush and large stones. They had left the last tree far below them.

The parrot was gone. He knew it at once, without even looking around, but he turned anyway, scanning the nearby vegetation for his green feathers. He felt no sense of alarm that the parrot was missing. It even seemed to him that somehow he had been expecting it. When the parrot had released his rope last night, it had seemed somehow to represent an ending.

He raised his eyes to the mountain slope above. The parrot would be there, among the tumbled boulders of the summit he could now see plainly in daylight. They had come even closer than he realized, a matter of a few hundred steps and no more. He began walking at once, picking his way carefully over the strewn stones which tended to roll under his hooves. He kept his eyes carefully on the ground and his mind free of speculation about the parrot. He was going to the summit of this mountain to see the Valley, if there was one, and then he would have to decide what to do. He did not even want to consider what would happen if he could not find the bird.

He reached a steep slope that passed between two solid walls of rock. He was forced to climb nearly on his two hind legs, and more than once he found himself in difficulties. He would have turned back to seek an easier route, but once he was committed it became impossible to descend safely. He fought his way up a last steep grade and found himself on a windy shelf of rock that was almost flat. He looked for the way upward, and then realized that there was none. He had reached the summit.

At the same instant he saw the parrot. He was sitting on the far edge of the rock shelf with his back to the donkey, apparently gazing out at the view to the east. The brisk wind stirred his plumage, exposing the many colours that lay beneath the green. He was very still, and, the donkey thought, he looked very small. "Bird!" called the donkey, but the parrot did not turn. The donkey ran in his direction, calling frantically, but the wind seemed to carry away his words. When he reached the parrot there was still no sign that he had heard, and it was not until he leaned over and nearly touched the parrot's head, that he moved at all.

The parrot turned his face toward the donkey. There was no recognition in his eyes. There was an expression of blankness that the donkey had never before seen on the face of a living creature. There was nothing to indicate that the donkey had any more substance than the wind that swept over them. The donkey started to speak, but the parrot turned his gaze back in the direction he had been facing. The donkey followed his gaze and looked out over what had been the Valley.

To the east was the shining vastness of the sea. The donkey knew this at once though he had never before seen it. To the north the mountains swung in a long arc, and turned in upon themselves to form a sheltered plain that sloped gradually to the sea. It was completely cut off from the rest of the land by the water and the mountains, as the parrot had said. But Men had defeated the mountains as they had defeated the creatures. They had arrived in great boats. One of them was visible now, a huge thing with machines on its back and many tiny swarming figures of Men. All around the beach stood huge mountains of white earth with flat tops on which more machines were building even as the donkey watched. The trees were all gone. The gentle breast of the land was pitted with craters and roads and the ugly yellow machines. There came to him, even at this distance, the sound of their work: The roar of motors and the shouts they made as they dug the heart out of the world.

The donkey could not guess what they were digging out of the ground and putting in their ship. It would be something which was of no interest to creatures. He looked at the scene, blurring his own sight, trying to imagine how it had been with deep grass and wild flowers and the sweet conversations of birds, but could not. The work of the Men had erased even the memory. It was not even possible to feel sorrow, and the donkey felt and understood the blankness that had altered and perhaps destroyed the parrot. He turned back to his companion, and as he did, the parrot took flight.

He rose, like a leaf plucked from the ground in a squall, rising swiftly into the air and hanging there for an instant before beginning a low trajectory toward the forest from which they had come. He flew with little effort, carried more by the wind than his own volition, and followed the steep contour of the mountain until he was lost in the distance.

The donkey stood stunned, looking after the green streak until it was gone. He felt the weight of things which he must consider. They were crowding the corridors of his mind, but he refused to let them enter. Without pausing to consider his actions he descended the rock shelf in the direction from which he had come. He went down slowly but without plan, keeping to the easy slopes until he found himself among the shrubs of the lower slopes. Even here he did not stop. Keeping his head down he walked, and slowly allowed himself to take in the events of the summit.

The parrot had flown! The donkey could not decide how long his companion must have known his wing feathers had regrown, but it meant, at least, that the parrot could have left him at any time during their long trek through the forest, but had decided to remain with him. This in turn meant that the parrot had genuinely thought to go with him into the Valley. His expedition alone this morning must have been only his impatience to set his eyes on the Valley before the exhausted donkey woke up.

The donkey stopped at the edge of the trees. He nibbled experimentally at the grass growing there, and found that despite everything, he had an appetite. He ate with concentration, struggling to digest the events of the morning. The sun rose higher, and the donkey watched passively as his own shadow slipped under him at midday. He was not surprised to see another, smaller shadow appear and circle around his. He raised his eyes to the sky knowing he would see the hawk.

Chapter Twelve

The hawk wheeled overhead in an easy orbit that carried him over the edge of the rock shelf and nearly to the trees on the downward slope of the mountain. The donkey watched. It occurred to him that the hawk would know where the parrot had gone, or, perhaps, had already disposed of him. The thought chilled him momentarily, but he concluded that if the hawk had recently caught and eaten prey, he wouldn't be here now, circling the sky.

But what did he want? Could it be that he had been following the donkey, and--not the parrot, after all? The donkey tried to see into the face of the hawk, but the distance was too great, and the sun caused him to blink. He dropped his eyes, and within seconds the hawk flew away, down the slope where the parrot had already gone. The donkey put the mystery of the hawk out of his mind. He was burdened enough already.

It was another hour before he acknowledged to himself that his path now lay back through the forest. He had no clear idea of where he must go, but, even though he could hardly admit it to himself, he felt the urge to return to the flat lands of Men. Rested and fed, he moved as soon as he realized he must, and without considering it further, he plunged into the forest once again.

He did not stop that day or during the night that followed, except once, briefly, to drink. When he was travelling, the momentum of his journey kept thoughts at bay, and for the present he could not bear to think about the parrot. Neither did he concern himself with jaguars, as if he was still travelling under the real or imagined protection of the parrot. He concentrated on the more difficult way down the slope, and neither his eyes nor his mind moved much beyond the next stretch of path.

Toward sundown of the following day he unexpectedly came upon the rubbish mountain. The fires were still smouldering on the tops of the garbage tips, but he had been too involved with his own steps to notice until he burst into the clearing. There was no sign of the mad boys, and the donkey was glad of this, although he surprised himself by feeling no fear of them. It seemed that too much had happened since his last encounter with them to allow his timidity to dominate.

It was on the wide road which led to the dump that the donkey felt his first wave of grief for the parrot. He was remembering how they had quarrelled about their route, and how he, the donkey, had resisted the advice of the parrot, who after all, had been right. At this moment he had the impression that the parrot was still riding his neck, and that if he turned suddenly enough, he would see him there, cockily viewing the world from donkey back. The fact that he would probably never see the parrot again came on him like a weight, and he resisted the impulse to part his lips and bray with frustration.

When he reached the lane they had followed, he went straight ahead without hesitation. He seemed not to fear meeting Men, or even their machines. He did not know where he was going, but he was going there without fear.

Even as he considered this fact, something occurred to him. It was as if the parrot were there, speaking to him inwardly. He felt the parrot's irony at the feeling of bravado he was displaying. He could almost hear a gently mocking voice telling him he was being foolish. He slowed his pace and made himself concentrate.

The parrot would not allow him to chase recklessly through the land of Men without any thought of where he was going. He would advise stealth, travel by night, and avoiding places where there were Men. The donkey was being reckless because he was sad and frustrated. He must come to his senses and take charge of the situation.

He would probably be captured again. Men, after all, were everywhere. But couldn't he decide where and by whom? An image of the kind woman crossed his mind, but was swept away by an impression of the parrot's scorn.

You cannot trust Men, the parrot would say. You must at least try to live without them, and if you failed--why, wasn't death preferable to life as their slave? Isn't that what the parrot would say, had in fact chosen? He might be lying dead even now, not free, but not enslaved.

As for the donkey, hadn't he already done many things he had never dreamt of before meeting the parrot? A sense of resolve stirred in him, and a feeling equally sweet, of defiance.

He found a cornfield and entered by pushing against a rotten post until it fell over. He ate his fill as the sky grew dark and then took to the road again. He ignored his fatigue, and felt with satisfaction the difference between driving oneself and being driven. The moon rose as he came to a narrow stream with high banks over which had been built a bridge. Intending to drink, he descended to the stream by a treacherous muddy path and walked ankle deep until he stood under the bridge. He noticed that from there he could not see the moon overhead, and it occurred to him that this might be a good place to pass the difficult daylight hours when Men were abroad. He was very tired, after all. There was water here, and just along the road were many cornfields. If he was careful, he might be able to stay here for a while. The idea seemed to grow more wonderful as he thought about it, and with pleasurable anticipation of a rest, he pressed himself against the bank under the planks of the bridge and stood still.

Sleep didn't come. He stamped, frustrated. He drank again and munched a little grass, but still he felt unsatisfied. It was several minutes before he was able to admit to himself that he missed the pressure of small talons on his neck. He exhaled a long, shuddering sigh and stared blindly upward at the bridge. Bird, he thought, where are you?

He was awakened by the sound of voices. Men were coming toward him along the road. They spoke in the coarse manner they used when there were no women with them, their voices huskier, laughing. They made loud stamping noises as they passed overhead. The donkey stood motionless though the flies were biting his ears, and he longed to swish his tail at them. Behind the Men came a boy, shoeless and silent, and a presence the donkey had not experienced in a long time. Another donkey! There were the half-forgotten sounds of a rope whip striking the hide of a creature, and the indolent gait of a donkey that was not too badly burdened. As they passed from view he heard the faint lines of the song all donkeys learn at their mothers' knee:

"When this here walking
Hurts worse than that whipping
This donkey's stopping."

Hardly noticing, he joined in under his breath. He was warm with excitement. It was a young male, not older than himself, though lighter in colour. He seemed healthy enough. Perhaps his master did not beat him much. Perhaps he was fed corn from that cornfield and did only light work. The inner voice of the parrot drew him up short. You are outsmarting yourself again, Ass, he could almost hear him say. Don't forget that Men are unreliable.

Still, he promised himself that he would go to this donkey and talk with him.

Tonight, when the Men were asleep. He seemed safe here under the bridge so far. It was only a matter of patience and caution.

He dozed again. He was awakened once as a woman passed over the bridge leading two goats. She was talking to them in the human language, and the donkey was sure that the goats--not known as intellectuals in any case--could not understand a single word she was saying. She went out of sight still talking, and the donkey dozed again. In the late afternoon he ate a little grass and lapped cautiously at the water. He was amusing himself by looking at the reflection of clouds on the surface of the water when he saw the image that had become so familiar to him-- the hawk turning slowly overhead. He inched forward and looked out from under the bridge. It seemed that the hawk dipped one wing as if to acknowledge his presence. From this distance it was possible to make out the bird's harsh features and his steely black eye that seemed to see everything on the earth. The donkey stood partly exposed, watching the hawk until suddenly he wheeled and descended swooping just a few feet over the donkey's head, emitting a shrill cry. Startled, the donkey jumped back, and just as he went under the sheltering overhang of the bridge, a truck appeared around the bend, travelling at speed. If he had not drawn back from the hawk's dive, he would certainly have been seen. He stood trembling in the shade until the truck rumbled past overhead, and it took him a few minutes before he was sure that the hawk, as strange as it seemed, had warned him.

Chapter Thirteen

It seemed to the donkey that night was taking forever to fall. Even when the light finally slipped westward over the trees, he waited. When the full serenade of frogs and cicadas began, he came out from under the bridge and began to walk cautiously down the road in the direction the other donkey had taken.

He struggled to keep his excitement from making him reckless. It seemed many long months since he had exchanged the news with another of his own breed, though it could not really have been more than a few weeks. Since he had met the parrot, time, as well as everything else, had been turned inside out. Even in the old days, when he belonged to the charcoal burner, it had been important to him to keep company with other donkeys when possible. Now that he was alone, it seemed vital.

Since he did not know where the donkey lived it was necessary for him to follow his nose and his ears. He walked quietly so that he could listen for sounds, and kept his nose high to receive scents carried in the night air. He found himself following a line of fence posts strung with a single strand of barbed wire. At the place where a lane led off to the right, he stopped, knowing he was at the entrance to a farm. He swivelled his ears forward and was rewarded with a sound so familiar that at first he did not recognize it: the rhythmic crunch of a donkey chewing grass. In seconds the sound stopped, and the donkey knew that he too had been heard. He turned down the lane and walked as softly as he could in the direction of the farm buildings.

The other donkey was standing at the verge of the lane a good distance from the sleeping Men. The donkey could make out his rather mottled hide as he approached. He was standing peacefully, as if waiting for someone. His front legs were held together by a rough rope hobble that kept him from walking. As he inched forward, he would be required to hop with both front hooves in a discouraging way. The donkey noted he had been seen when the other suddenly turned to face him and called out nervously, "Who's that?"

"A friend," the donkey said, containing his excitement. He went forward and stood still so that the other could examine him.

"You are a donkey," said the other.

"Very observant," said the donkey. The irony seemed lost on the other.

"Whose are you?" he asked.

"Nobody's," said the donkey calmly, but the very word made him want to shout it to the night.

The other resumed his grazing, plucking rather formally at the grass. The donkey joined him, more out of convention than appetite.

"Well," he said after a moment, "Aren't you going to ask me what I'm doing here, without a master?"

"Yes, I suppose so," the other said without curiosity.

"I'm on a journey," said the donkey. The other nodded politely. The donkey found this frustrating.

"Go ahead," he prompted impatiently, "Ask me where I'm going."

"Okay. Where are you going?"

"I'm searching for a place where there are no Men," the donkey said, wondering at the statement even as he made it. The other donkey did not reply, the donkey noticed, and was no longer even looking at him.

"Well," said the donkey impatiently, "What do you think about that?"

"About what?" said the other without lifting his face from the grass.

"About looking for a place where there are no Men," the donkey snapped, resisting an impulse to nip at his companion's ears.

The other looked at him. "I don't quite follow you, he said carefully. I'm sorry."

The donkey's head spun. He had planned to tell the other about his meeting with the parrot, their journey across the world, the adventures, and the sad ending when the parrot disappeared. But he was mute with frustration to see that this other donkey was not even interested. He would certainly not understand.

"I see that you do not believe me," he said when he had recovered his composure.

The other shrugged. "What do I know of these things? What you have told me is impossible, so I have no opinion."

The donkey felt something like rage. He went forward until his face was inches from his companion's.

"Listen to me," he hissed, placing a hoof on the connection strand of the hobble between the other's legs.

"If you raise your foot now, and pull just a little, you can get out of this thing," he said.

"Why?" asked the other, with a look of honest bafflement.

"To get free," said the donkey. "Like me."

"But why?" persisted the other.

"Because," began the donkey wildly, "It is better. It is much better to be free, that's all."

"But where would I go? What would I do?" said the other. "Besides, I am sure the farmer wouldn't like it."

"Forget the farmer!" the donkey shouted. "Come away with me!"

"That's impossible," said the other firmly. He looked about him primly, giving the donkey an unspoken reproof for raising his voice. He seemed to study the donkey momentarily, then began talking in an exaggeratedly soothing style, which inflamed the donkey even further.

"You're asleep!" he spat. "And you don't even know it." He shook his head to clear it,

and was startled to see the other back away
in fear.

"I am not mad," he said. He turned away,
toward the road, feeling desolate. He
wondered before the words were fully
spoken if they were true, and if they were
not, if he would even know himself. He
walked briskly away, leaving the other so
completely that he was startled to hear his
voice as he turned out of sight, saying,

"Have a pleasant journey."

When he reached the road he turned to
the right and began to walk briskly, ignoring
the night sounds. He tramped hard upon
the dust as if it were the protests of an
ignorant donkey. His frustration didn't leave
him until the first rays of the sun lit up a
cornfield on a slowly rising slope. He
thought for the first time then of food, and
turned and stepped over a sagging bit of
wire and went into the field to eat. He
ripped some ripe cobs from their stalks and
ate hungrily until he was satisfied and did

not stop to think until he saw that he had trampled a large area of the field. A farmer would discover this damage, he realized, and would be angry. The thought made him happy. When he went back onto the road he realized that he had not only been walking all night, but that he had been walking in the direction of the city. Before he had a chance to consider this fact, a shadow crossed his feet and he looked up, as he must have known he would all along, to greet the hawk.

Chapter Fourteen

The hawk landed gracefully in the road in front of the donkey, folded his wings with great precision and fixed him with his penetrating black eyes. He was smaller than he seemed when soaring with spread wings, and except for the patch of red feathers at his pail, he was the dun colour of the soil.

The donkey experienced an eerie feeling of familiarity with this strange bird, though they had never actually met. The black eyes seemed to scan his mind as well as his form. They were never still, but restlessly examined everything they met. The donkey shifted uncomfortably under his scrutiny. As keen as they were, the eyes held no message. They seemed only to work in one direction. The donkey broke the silence.

"Why have you been following me?" he surprised himself by saying.

The hawk did not answer, but his feathers moved in a barely perceptible shrug.

"I thought you were after the parrot," the donkey continued, "To eat him."

The hawk gave a rasping laugh. "That old sack of bones?" he said in a shrill but powerful voice, "I doubt if he would have made a tender meal for my grandfather."

"Then why were you always overhead?"

The hawk shifted his weight but did not reply. He continued to peer at the donkey with that combination of studiousness and indifference which made it clear that he considered all conversation optional.

"What did you want?" the donkey said, allowing his impatience to show.

The hawk lifted one taloned foot and stretched the sharp claws. The donkey could not help a sense of relief that it had been the parrot and not this bird of prey he had been carrying.

"Why did you carry the parrot?" the hawk asked suddenly.

"Because he could not fly." The answer, he could see, had not been satisfactory. There was an impression of disapproval from the hawk even though he did not alter his air of detachment.

"Where were you trying to go?"

"To the Valley. Over the mountains. The parrot said that there were no Men there."

He expected the hawk to scoff, but he merely intensified his concentration on the donkey's eyes. It occurred to the donkey that the hawk wanted to know something for which he was unable to frame a question.

"Do you know what happened to him?" the donkey asked shyly.

"Of course," said the hawk.

"Will you tell me?"

The hawk raised his gaze momentarily to the sky

"I will do better than that," he said, opening his broad wings, "I will show you."

He launched himself forward and was instantly aloft. He circled once above the donkey and then rose higher and headed west, the direction of the city.

"Wait!" the donkey cried, "I can't travel now, in the daylight!" But the hawk soared on, oblivious or indifferent. The donkey hesitated, but seeing the small figure grow fainter, started down the road in a half trot, not for the first time under the influence of a wilful bird.

It seemed that the hawk knew well the problem of the donkey's capture, for as he led the donkey through the morning, he found himself always just out of the sight of Men. Sometimes the hawk changed direction without warning, causing the donkey to veer off at right angles down a different track. Once he swooped low and gave one of his metallic cries, indicating that the donkey should take cover in some trees. He did, and a truck with two Men passed by without seeing him. He began to relax, and once again his steps became mechanical.

The journey lasted all day. The donkey was thirsty and hungry by late afternoon, but the hawk kept up the pace until nearly dark. They were nearing the city, as the unmistakable signs of Men began to increase. The donkey lost his semi-conscious rhythm, and began to worry in earnest. Once the hawk actually disappeared from sight for a moment, and the donkey felt an old panic return. But after a few second, the hawk reappeared, hanging patiently just over the trees ahead, and the donkey pushed onward.

At dusk, the hawk swooped low and spoke to the donkey from a hanging spiral overhead . "You should rest now," he called. "Turn down the next lane and wait there for me. I am going to hunt." He rose so swiftly that the donkey could not answer.

The next lane took him to a small farm behind a coffee grove. The farmhouse had been burnt, and the place was deserted. There was a small shed, meant for housing farm animals. He looked inside cautiously, but could see no signs of life. Behind the ruin of the house was a small stream, with a well-worn path made by human feet. He descended and drank deeply before returning to the shed. It had a grass roof, and the donkey nibbled at the thatch as he passed. He was too tired to eat, he found. The building was dark and cool. He settled himself against the palm boards, and before sleeping thought wonderingly how easily he had come to adapt to strange places and circumstances that hardly suited a donkey at all.

The night came and deepened, and the hawk did not return. The donkey slept. He dreamed of the parrot, circling high overhead as the hawk had done. The donkey called and called for him to come down, but he would not. He seemed to be insisting that the donkey should fly up into the air to meet him. "But I can't fly!" the donkey cried out over and over. At last his own voice woke him, and he found himself confronted with the ironic gaze of the hawk, who had arrived silently and perched on a beam of the shed.

"It is time to go to your friend the parrot," he said emotionlessly. "We must pass through the streets of the city now, so you must be fast. Do you understand?"

"Yes."

"Follow me carefully. I will lead you directly to where he is."

"But where is he? Is he all right?"

The hawk shrugged. He shot off his perch soundlessly and out the door of the barn. The donkey followed as if pulled by an invisible rope. He did not think of where he was going. It was far too late for that.

They had indeed been close to the city, the donkey saw as he set off. He found himself travelling the same streets they had taken after their escape from the poor family. People were just beginning to stir. Fires were being lit. There was the sound of coughing, shouts and crying infants that the donkey associated with the homes of Men. Strangely, no one seemed interested in him as he passed, keeping one eye on the road and the other on the hawk hovering overhead.

The buildings got closer together, and open fields yielded to small garden plots, and even these finally disappeared. The road surface hardened, and began to hold cars, a few of which were moving sluggishly. The sun cleared the trees and illuminated the pall of smoke and dust that seemed to hang forever in the streets. All around him were the sickly odour of Men and their machines, and the donkey ignored these. The hawk was stepping up the pace, forcing him into a jerky trot, and there was no time to reflect on the fact that he was heading now into the thicket of Men and their menace.

He met a crossing road and crossed without looking either way. The blare of a car horn shook him, and he lurched as a truck screeched to a halt just short of his flank. A Man extended his head from the cab and shouted a curse at him. The donkey plunged ahead into even denser crowds of Men.

Suddenly the street widened, became a large open space filled with Men and vehicles. It was a bewildering spectacle of tables with goods heaped atop, women surrounded by children as they sat behind piles of vegetables, baskets and cloth. There was human noise of the type which made Men dance when they were drunk, scratched out on drums and wooden flutes. The hawk settled into a tight circle exactly circumscribing the square. When he saw the donkey stop at the entrance, he swooped low over a tent in one corner, at the same time letting out one of his grating cries.

The donkey went forward, to the annoyance of people who found themselves in the way of his blundering movements. Like an automaton he went through the crowds, who parted with surprising ease. The hawk had indicated a single spot at the far corner, and as unlikely as it might seem, the parrot must be there. Oblivious, the donkey put his head down and ran.

Chapter Fifteen

Rudolfo lifted the crude cage from the shelf behind his stall and gave it a ceremonious swipe with his bandanna. He held the cage aloft as if it held precious stones instead of the rather bedraggled-looking parrot. With his free hand he folded into quarters the money the American woman had paid him and thrust it deep into the tight pockets of his grimy trousers, under the protective bulge of his belly. The *gringa* took the cage and pressed her face against the bars.

"Pretty Polly," she cooed to the parrot, which was hunched obliviously against the opposite wall. One yellow eye appeared briefly and looked uncomprehendingly at the rouged cheeks of the woman and then shut again wearily. Rudolfo cleared his throat noisily, distracting the woman from the fact that the bird looked to be at death's door. He was eager to have the woman leave in her hired car before the bird collapsed. Once she actually left the market with her purchase, there would be no recourse. He made theatrical gestures of invitation, moving toward the dusty Chevrolet which was occupied by a bored-looking driver. The woman followed, holding the cage unsteadily away from her body. Rudolfo took it from her as she squeezed her bulk onto the back seat.

A glance at the parrot told him it was none too soon. The bird was swaying on its perch. It had been brought to him by boys who caught it, so they said, without effort as it sat in a guava tree. It was an old bird, Rudolfo could see by its feathers. It also must be ill, since it had refused to eat or drink since he had brought it to the market, the day before yesterday. It had not even been necessary to clip its wing, because the bird showed no interest in escape. He had sold it at the first opportunity to this

American woman, who miraculously had failed to notice its condition, even in comparison to the several other, more vigorous parrots in Rudolfo's stall. Now she reached out with chubby arms for the cage, making wet smacking noises with her lips that reminded him that he must remember to buy food for his two pigs on his way home this evening.

Rudolfo shut the door and gave a half-hearted salute to the driver, who leaned forward to start the car. Rudolfo became aware that there was something amiss only when he heard the hoof beats behind him. He turned to see a donkey charging headlong toward the stall, with whites showing all around his eyes and flecks of foam at his lips. He leapt backwards and the donkey crashed into the table, knocking it over and spilling its display of wood carvings and baskets. Rudolfo watched stunned as the animal wheeled about and let out a bray at high volume. Its eyes moved wildly about the shelves and then seemed to fixate on the car. It lunged at the rear window and seemed about to put its head through the glass. The woman screamed. She was hugging the cage tightly to her breast. The parrot had opened one eye a slit, but alone seemed uninterested in the events unfolding around it. The driver had dropped his cigarette from his lips and was cursing and sweeping live cinders from his lap. The donkey spun again and came to rest in front of the car, blocking its way, and stood facing Rudolfo with its wild expression.

"It is mad," Rudolfo heard himself say. "Rabies."

The driver let go the ignition. The woman was still making sounds, though Rudolfo could not say whether they were words in her language or merely terrified grunts. He himself was shaking, but he decided to take charge of the situation. He lurched forward toward the donkey, waving his arms. The donkey blinked but did not change his position. Rudolfo raised his fist as if to strike, and the donkey's eyes opened wider, but still he did not move. Rudolfo was filled with further uncertainty. His diagnosis of rabbles seemed all the more likely. As he turned to find a stick with which to hit the beast, he heard the driver hoot the powerful horn of the American car. It was a high, irritating sound, like warped trumpets, that jarred Rudolfo's nerves, but he saw at once that the donkey was not moved. He found a length of heavy cane that he used for a tent pole and brandished it at the donkey. There was no response other than a slight further widening of the beast's eyes. Rudolfo had never known a donkey not to flinch from a stick, and it filled him with fear. Without thinking, he struck at the donkey. The heavy cane landed on the donkey's head, making a loud noise.

"Go, you idiot!" shouted Rudolfo. He struck again, this time on the side of the donkey's neck, but still there was no response--other than a slight reflex jerk. The donkey regarded him with wide eyes that seemed not to see him at all.

"Go, damn you," Rudolfo cursed again and embarked on a furious volley of blows. The car horn sounded continuously, and a crowd gathered, at first subdued, but then beginning to laugh at the sight. The woman had stopped her wailing and had begun to shout in her foreign language, words which Rudolfo could not understand, but which were clearly oaths. He felt sweat pour into his eyes and stopped briefly his beating of the donkey to wipe his face with a bandanna.

"Start the car!" he shouted to the driver. The engine roared into life, startling the crowd, but not moving, the donkey whose eyes had left the face of his tormentor Rudolfo and now stared into the car itself. Rudolfo jumped back.

"Go on!" he screamed to the driver, waving his arm maniacally. "Drive! Run over the son of a bitch!"

The car lurched slightly as the driver put it into gear. His face was a mask of resolve. Through the windscreen Rudolfo could see his jaw set as he let out the clutch and moved forward into the side of the donkey.

Chapter Sixteen

The donkey felt the car engine start. It throbbed into hot, noisy life inches from his side. The sound filled his ears and his muscles screamed at him to break and run. The fat Man had stopped beating him, and the stars that had appeared before his eyes cleared so that he caught a glimpse of the parrot sitting with eyes still tightly shut in his cage in the back of the car.

The car lurched, and the roar increased. The donkey planted his feet and tried to ignore the sound by willing the parrot to look at him.

"Bird!" he called, but the parrot either could not or would not hear. He seemed turned inward, in that withdrawal that in an animal indicates the nearness of death.

The fat Man shouted again, and suddenly the car was touching his ribs. The sharp metal nose pressed painfully, and the power of the machine made his legs tremble. He set his jaw and willed himself to grow roots in the road like a tree. I am a tree, he thought, and I will not move.

The car inched forward. The donkey felt his feet slide on the hard surface. He locked his knees and leaned against the force of the car, but he could not get a purchase. The roar of the engine and the screaming Men were a single deafening note in his ears, like the wail of a strong wind. As he slid slowly sideways, the sound seemed to leave him. He knew he was going to fall, to be pushed onto his side and crushed by the wheels of the car. He felt no fear, only a regret that the parrot would not, even now, answer him. Even that didn't matter, and if he died preventing them taking the parrot, then that was how things were. He would not move.

His left rear leg caught on something and turned. He felt himself heeling over. The silver ornament of the car rose above his eyes just as he saw the head of the parrot swivel toward him. One eye, opened, a yellow window darkened with despair. It widened, and in the curious slow descent he was making toward the pavement, a single clawed foot reached through the bars of the cage and sought the latch. As he fell, he knew that the parrot was free, taking wing through the fat outstretched fingers of the woman toward the driver. There was a hoarse scream as the shiny bumper of the car covered him, and then the car came to rest.

"Ass!" came the shrill voice of the parrot. "Come out, Ass!"

The parrot appeared overhead, flapping furiously, a green blur against the heavens. The crowd had fallen silent in their astonishment, and the donkey could hear the beating of his wings.

The donkey scrambled against the asphalt, legs wheeling helplessly before gaining traction against the tyre of the car. He slithered free of the bumper and lurched unsteadily to his feet while the crowd backed away in awe. He felt the familiar grip of talons on his spine.

"Go, Ass!" the parrot hissed. "Go like hell!"

The crowd parted before them like pigeons, and the donkey ran, oblivious to what lay ahead. He crashed through and over the market stalls scattering goods and tethered chickens and excited children like straw. The good air of freedom reached his nostrils and filled him like a wind. He raced through the streets in the direction from which he had come, and did not slow down until the traffic thinned and the astonished faces of Men became fewer and fewer and finally vanished altogether. Soon fields and sky surrounded them. Almost without knowing it, he turned in at the lane which led to the farm and went directly to the barn. It wasn't until he stood in the cool shade that he became aware of the effort he had expended, and for the first time in his life felt the need to sink to his knees. He lay winded in the straw, feeling the parrot silently dismount, and let sleep take him.

He dozed fitfully, moving restlessly between dreams and the shady reality of the barn. He got to his feet, determined to speak with the parrot, but fell asleep again. His head was swimming with visions and memories that faded when he opened his eyes. He struggled with the charcoal burner and turned again to the kind woman who had stroked his side. As night fell, he opened his eyes to see the parrot perched easily on a cross beam, watching him with concern.

"Bird," he said weakly, "I was dreaming. I thought I saw you with the hawk over there, by the door."

"That was no dream. The hawk was here."

"Did you talk with him?"

"Yes."

"What did he want?"

The parrot didn't speak at once, but sat quietly looking at the donkey out of one yellow eye.

"He wanted what we all want, Ass," he said at last. "He wanted to understand."

"Does he understand now?"

The parrot fluttered down onto the donkey's spine, and placed his talons in the exact spot he preferred. The sensation was soothing to the donkey.

"There's good tall grass by the stream," the parrot said. "Care for a bite before dark?" His voice sounded subdued, almost gentle. The donkey thought again of the dead look he had seen in his friend's eyes on the mountain, and again, of the despairing figure in his cage waiting to be sold in the market. It seemed that that emptiness was now banished, but so, perhaps was his raucous confidence. He went out into the cooling air and ate grass in silence. The parrot was still.

"It is peaceful here, Bird," he said after drinking at the stream.

"Yes, it is."

"There is grass, and there are wild fruits for you, and plenty of water."

"So there is."

"The barn is shady by day, and at night there is no one about."

"True," said the parrot mildly.

"Then, maybe..." he began, but even as the words left his mouth, he disowned them.

"No," he said quietly.

"No," agreed the parrot.

They stood quietly in the darkness, listening to the swelling song of the night beings, who still lived in the illusion that there were no Men. It was they who had learned to admit that there was no avoiding Men, and no defeating them, either. They felt oddly comforted by this admission, for, though there were no answers, at least they understood the question. After a few moments the donkey returned to the barn and slept.

He awoke after some hours. It was still dark, but he could see the compact green form of the parrot through the gloom.

"Are you awake?" asked the parrot. He seemed to be staring fixedly at the donkey.

"Yes."

"The first time I asked you that, you said you didn't know."

"Now I know," said the donkey. "I'm awake."

"I wanted to say something, Ass."

"Okay."

"Thank you."

"For what?"

"For coming back for me," said the parrot softly, in a voice which spoke volumes. It was clear, and somehow had regained the quality of birdsong which the cynicism of captivity had obscured.

"Bird, don't..." said the donkey, embarrassed.

"I was a goner there, Ass, and you know it."

"You had a shock, Bird."

"I had given up. When it came to the crunch, I didn't have it. But you did."

"Had what?"

"I don't know what to call it. It is something we creatures need if we are to survive. The wild creatures don't seem to have it. When Men move in, they just seem to die. But you, who have no history, born-- pardon me, Ass--a slave, you have it, and you saved me with it."

"I didn't know what else to do."

"So you did it. You challenged the machine. You refused to budge. And you, well, you woke me up."

"Then we're even," said the donkey, and there was no need to explain.

In the morning they behaved shyly with each other, as if the confessions of the night could not stand the daylight.

The donkey grazed furtively behind the barn, once more aware of the risks of being seen by Men. The parrot was silent, content to sit astride the donkey while he ate the grass. It was the donkey who finally voiced the question that had hung in the air unmentioned.

"Well, Bird, now where do we go?"

"I was going to ask you the same question."

"Well," said the donkey, "Let's see. We could stay here for a while, just to get our strength back." He glanced over his shoulder at the parrot's impassive face.

"We could go back to the forest." He paused and waited for the parrot's reaction, but there was none. "But I don't like it much. There's no really good grass and there are jaguars." He returned to eating the young grass, waiting for the parrot to speak. When several minutes passed without a response, he said,

"Or we could just admit that we need Men, and let ourselves get captured again.

"That's going too far, damn it!" said the parrot. Men may be inescapable, but I, at least, do not need them."

"Okay, not need them, but, well, we are forced to deal with them."

There was an even longer silence, which he feared would end with an expression of wrath from the parrot, but when his companion spoke again, it was in a calm, even resigned tone.

"You are right, Ass" he said, and did not say, for once.

"So where does that leave us?"

"It means....it means get captured by the right Man," said the donkey boldly. "Only we choose the time and the place."

He bent his head to the grass again, to avoid embarrassment, and in this way failed to see the smile on the face of the parrot.

"You are essentially right, Ass. We must indeed find ourselves a congenial captivity, if such a thing exists." he paused. "But we do not need Men. It is the other way around." He smiled secretively. "And then, we may have other work to do..."

The donkey felt the onset of a familiar giddiness from trying to follow the parrot's reasoning, and therefore allowed the words to disperse like motes of dust in a shaft of daylight, beautiful and fleeting. He turned away from the visionary eyes.

"At least," said the donkey, "We know we must avoid the charcoal burner."

"There is no charcoal burner," said the parrot.

"Pardon?"

"The hawk told me," said the parrot, obviously savouring his news. "The farmer, you remember, the one who we, er, made sick--well, he must have been in a bad temper the morning Luis arrived. He would have been still feeble, I guess. You

188

remember, he had a gun. Anyway, the charcoal burner was probably drunk, and, well..."

The donkey stood still, waiting for a rush of triumph to overwhelm him. Nothing came. The truth was that he had stopped fearing the charcoal burner long, so long ago that he did not even remember stopping. All that remained was a feeling unfamiliar in his breast. It felt like pity, but, of course, that was impossible.

During the afternoon the parrot remained silent, in a mood which the donkey recognized as scheming. He kept his eyes fixed over the trees, and evaded the donkey's questions. At last, frustrated, the donkey demanded a reply.

"Well?" he said impatiently, "Are you planning our future?"

"Perhaps," said the parrot distantly.

"Perhaps," mimicked the donkey sarcastically, "you wouldn't mind giving me a clue, since I am presumably involved."

"I will do that, Ass, certainly," said the parrot with a broad smile. "All in good time. But first, I would like to ask you to do a little something for me."

"What?" asked the donkey suspiciously.

"Do you remember when I was wounded, and you had to bend way down to allow me to get to the ground? You bent your legs and stuck your neck out in front, do you remember?"

"Yes, but what--"

"Will you do it for me?" the parrot was oozing charm.

"What, now?"

"Yes, now. That's right, Ass," he said, as the donkey rather stiffly complied. "Only a bit more smoothly, with long motions. Try it again."

The donkey complied, embarrassed and mystified.

"Are you going to get down?" he asked from the semi-supine posture he was being made to hold.

"Not now. Now listen, Ass, when the dogs were chasing us, you went up on two legs and sort of turned around in the air. Can you do it?"

"I don't know if I can do it without being scared."

"Look! A jaguar!" shouted the parrot.

"Very funny. All right, I'll try." He went clumsily up onto his hind legs and turned with difficulty.

"Good!" said the parrot. "Keep it up!"

"Bird, what are we doing?" the donkey complained, only half serious.

"Just trust me, Ass," said the parrot, without a trace of irony.

Chapter Seventeen

Dolores left the cathedral by the main door, blinking a little in the harsh afternoon light of the square. The cool intimacy of the chapel of the Virgin evaporated instantly, and she clutched her blouse together as if clutching at the garment of the Queen of Heaven herself, whose mercy she had been beseeching as she knelt on the tiles of the ancient floor. There had been no response from the statue which represented the Virgin in this world of squalor and traffic, but Dolores had not expected any. She had been content to lay her case before the Divine Mother once again, before surrendering to necessity. She wanted it to be that on the day she became a whore she first knelt in prayer at the Virgin's feet.

It was with this fading sense of the holy that she came into the roiling tumult of the square to find Epifanio. In his bitterness at life he had been refusing to set foot inside a church since the accident, and their son, though only six, followed suit. In the boy's eyes, Dolores feared she could see the beginning of a cynicism that exceeded even that of her husband, which would rob him of his childhood, and perhaps even his life.

Epifanio was inclined beneath a distressed sycamore tree that was slowly dying from its assault of urination and cuts from the pen knives of hoodlum boys. He had exposed the ugly pink stump of his amputated leg and was brandishing it aggressively at the crowds which passed, as if to punish them for the humiliation he experienced through having to beg. Perhaps for this reason there was no money at all in the inverted hat beside his leg, as they had had not even a penny to put in to prime the pump. Marco sat unnaturally still beside him, and met the gaze of passers-by with a coldness unknown to most children.

She hurried across the square. The boy looked up when she approached, but Epifanio did not acknowledge her arrival. Perhaps he knew that she had arranged to meet Conchita at her whore's bar this afternoon. She had been promised a "respectable" first client by the madam, to break her more gently in to her new life. Epifanio would not know the details, but he would know all the same, and perhaps the unusually bitter look on his face was directed inward because he was still just slightly more interested in remaining alive than in retaining his wife's honour. The boy might actually have overheard her talking to her neighbour, but the flatness of his eyes indicated that he was leaving behind a state which mere feelings could affect. She took his hand momentarily and squeezed its dry smallness into her own, and her prayer leapt again to her lips.

There was the sound of indrawn breath. Dolores opened her eyes to see the face of her son staring in amazement. She turned, and from the denseness of the plaza crowd an apparition appeared. It was a donkey, to all appearances the one who had briefly been theirs before escaping. It ran purposefully up to Epifanio and stopped, turning to face the crowd, which was gathering like pigeons around tossed crumbs of bread. Riding on the donkey's neck was a parrot and, though she was not conscious of having seen it before, it looked strangely familiar. Epifanio sat bolt upright against the tree, and Marco scrambled to his feet.

Beginning faintly, but rising swiftly to volume, someone sang. It was a well-known piece from the Mexican revolution called Adelita, sung in a pure but reedy tenor, with the hint of a guitar chord in the background. Dolores looked around before realizing that the song was coming from the parrot, and as she watched, the donkey, very agilely, began to dance. The crowd fell back; there was a murmur which rippled through their ranks and then died away in attention to the song. The donkey stood first on his back legs and then bowed forward, intermingling the steps with a sideways prancing motion that may not have been in perfect time to the music, but which swept away all criticism by its grace and humour. The tempo picked up; the crowd formed a perfect swelling circle around the animals and the small amazed family. Another verse was started. The donkey danced faster still. His movements were quicker and more refined as he responded to the delight of the crowd. The song reached a climax, and the voice of the parrot seemed to grow and include an accordion in its reaches. It ended on a long high wail, and in the instant following the last note there was a silence never before heard in the busy square. Then, like raindrops at the start of a shower came the first claps of applause. It swelled into a roar, coupled with cries of "encore" and then the clink of silver as coins began, slowly at first and then in a cascade, to fill Epifanio's upturned hat. The donkey bowed, and the parrot's head swivelled to look at them as they stood helplessly receiving their bounty.

Dolores turned from this gift to find her real miracle, granted as she knew it would be by the Virgin; the sheen of tears on the face of her son, who appeared, for the first time in months, a little boy.

Chapter Eighteen

The donkey stood waiting in the brand new shed the people had made for him beside their house. He nibbled at a fresh bundle of hay the boy had cut for him and laid beside his water trough. The last sounds of the family had died away for the night, and he knew that soon the parrot would leave his cage and join him. He heard a fluttering in the dark as the parrot squeezed over the bamboo door. Within seconds he was mounted in his familiar perch on the donkey's neck.

"Does it hurt?" were the first words of the parrot.

He was referring to the fact that the donkey had been rebranded during the afternoon, and a certain charred aroma still clung to him.

"Not as much as a gunshot, or being run over by a car," said the donkey. "How is your wing?"

"I've had it clipped so often that it doesn't matter at all." He nestled more closely to the donkey, ostensibly for better balance. The donkey, who got lonely too sometimes, understood. The parrot was in the habit these days of staying with the donkey until dawn and then returning undetected to his cage. They both felt that the boy of the family was aware of this, but had chosen to say nothing for his own reasons.

"The boy looks a bit better, doesn't he?" said the donkey. "Less sort of dirty, I mean."

"He's all right, for a Man child," the parrot said grudgingly. "But I still think he was one of those boys that attacked us at the garbage mountain."

"It doesn't matter now," said the donkey. The parrot grunted his assent.

"What are they talking about these days?" the donkey asked.

"They are planning a trip to the Capital to show us off. On a stage, not in the street."

"I hope they don't," grumbled the donkey.

"You're still very conservative, you know," jibed the parrot. "Why not go to the Capital?"

"It probably means riding in a car or something, said the donkey.

"Oh, and the woman wants to bring a priest here, to bless us," said the parrot, changing the subject.

"What does that entail?"

"Just a little water sprinkled on your ears. And some praying. They're very big on that sort of thing, you know."

The donkey muttered half-heartedly. It was really difficult to get worried about things these days. He plucked a particularly sweet stem of grass from the pile and drew it in luxuriously. Sometimes, contentment seemed not impossible.

"So we'll go on like this for a while, don't you agree, Ass?" the parrot said after a while. "It is not so bad, all things considered."

The donkey grunted.

"By day we will dance and sing for the people, and they will never know that we are not merely unconscious creatures. But by night, perhaps..."

"By night, what?" said a third voice from the darkness at the rear of the shed. It belonged to a stray cat, who was taking advantage of the family's good fortune by insinuating himself slowly into the orbit of their home. He moved forward, so that the donkey could see him. He had one of those unfortunate feline faces in which the markings had been so distributed as to obscure any expression that may have appeared there. In recent days he had been following them like a shadow, apparently fascinated with them.

"What will you do at night, Bird?" he repeated in that nasally unpleasant cat voice which makes them so unloved by other creatures.

But it was the donkey who answered.

"At night," he said, "We shall speak the truth."

THE END